Love Restored

Lieze Gerber

CRIMSON ROMANCE
Avon, Massachusetts

This edition published by
Crimson Romance
an imprint of F+W Media, Inc.
10151 Carver Road, Suite 200
Blue Ash, Ohio 45242

www.crimsonromance.com

ISBN 10: 1-4405-5440-4
ISBN 13: 978-1-4405-5440-7
eISBN 10: 1-4405-5441-2
eISBN 13: 978-1-4405-5441-4

Dedication

TO ALL THE PEOPLE AND PETS WHO SUPPORTED ME ON THIS CRAZY, WONDERFUL JOURNEY, AND TO EVERY ROMANCE WRITER OUT THERE.

Chapter One

"Oh come on, Rachel, you owe it to yourself. It's been three years since that wretched husband of yours ran away, and you've been working nonstop since then."

Recognizing the familiar ring of determination in her friend's voice, Rachel rolled her eyes to the ceiling and stood from her desk to close her office door. She returned, crossed her legs, and sat back in her executive leather chair with a soft sigh. From past experiences, she knew Tina wouldn't easily be swayed.

"Just think of it—warm sun, fabulous food, excellent wine . . . and there may even be a handsome French gentleman to enchant you," Tina continued. Rachel laughed at Tina's glib remark.

"So?" Tina's question sounded in her ear.

Blissful—a week in the south of France. Rachel deliberated and twirled a long coil of hair around her finger at the memories of the grand old house in Cassis she'd helped renovate. The image of long, lazy lunches in the shade of the massive plane trees in the back garden brought a soft smile to Rachel's lips. But she had so much on her plate right now.

"Come on, Rachel, you haven't been down here for ages." Tina continued her slow dismantling of Rachel's defenses.

"Tina, you know that's not true. I was there last year after we finished the renovation. The kids fell in love with Arianne . . . we had too much rosé wine—"

"That, my dear Rachel, was work. I'm inviting you for a break."

"Thanks, Tina, but I just can't take a week off right now. I'm working on two large proposals, both due by the end of the month." She glanced through the thick glass wall of her office at the group of people in the meeting room directly across from her.

By tomorrow, they would need her input on the design—a design she'd hoped to finish this afternoon.

"Nonsense, Rachel. You work much too hard." Then the tone in Tina's voice changed as she said, almost pleading, "You've been isolating yourself ever since Stuart left you and the twins. I worry about you . . . we worry about you." Tina paused and then continued, "I miss my Rachel." Finally, in a small voice, she added, "And besides, if you have to work, why can't you bring your blessed work with you?"

Rachel exhaled slowly, contemplating Tina's words. It all sounded so tempting, and a break from the bleak London weather would be heavenly. And Tina was right—the last three years had been grueling. Rebuilding her life, as a single mother at the age of twenty-six, was not easy. But she had to do it, for herself and for her twin babies, Mia and Iain. They were the reason why she'd resumed her once-stellar career as an architect and worked so doggedly at building this fledgling business with her business partner—to recreate a life where her children would be secure again.

Irritated, Rachel shifted in her chair at the unpleasant memory of her gutless husband's selfish words on that horrible day, when he walked out of her life.

And so, when Stuart boarded that aging Boeing 747 for Nairobi, he left her with nothing—no love, no hope, no money, and no way to contact him. To her dismay, she later found that he did leave her with something—his outstanding bills. The credit card statements for new photographic equipment, outstanding rent on his studio, and three unpaid installments on their leased Volvo—all landed on her desk.

She struggled to sell their house, the incomplete basement blaring "desperate seller" from below. Eventually the nightmare ended when a newlywed couple fell in love with the house. Anxious to minimize the disruption to their lives, Rachel settled on the first apartment she could find—actually, Tina found it. Probably too spacious for what Rachel needed, but it was renovated to her taste, and conveniently located in Putney. In that apartment, Rachel created a new home.

While all this happened around her, Rachel was well aware of her commitment to Peter and their new business partnership—and the new career she was carving out for herself. She soon found that their frail business venture was consuming every spare hour of her time. Her body learned to cope with less sleep, and her social life came to a jarring halt. Weekends and evenings became a carefully orchestrated balancing act between caring for the twins, the demoralizing task of running a household as a single mother, and catching up on an ever-increasing workload at the office.

She bit her lower lip while she rationalized. A short break in sunny Provence would give her some fresh perspectives—new ideas. Besides, her parents had been nagging her to take some time off as well, though she suspected the idea of having the twins all to themselves was their true incentive. She smiled inwardly at the thought of how, at three years of age, the twins had already mastered the fine art of manipulating her parents. A couple of days bonding with Granny and Grandpa might be a real treat for them.

Oh, hell, why not?

"Fine, but just for a couple of days," Rachel relented on impulse, and laughed aloud as she pulled her head away at Tina's excited whoop of joy shrilling over the telephone.

Chapter Two

The weather was balmy with a light breeze when Rachel's flight from Gatwick landed at Marseille airport late Tuesday afternoon the following week. As she stepped from the terminal building into the warm afternoon sun, Tina waved her straw hat at her where she was waiting, double-parked in the taxi zone. She gripped her silver, wheeled suitcase and hurried toward Tina's little red Italian convertible, enjoying the wonderful effect of the heat on her face where the late afternoon sun touched her skin. "Now if only I can get out of these jeans and jacket and into a light summer dress," she mumbled, making her way through the crowd.

"Oh, how I missed this—the sun, the blue skies." She laughed and hugged Tina. Radiant in a lilac linen shift dress, Tina flipped her honey-brown hair from her face, her eyes dancing with delight at seeing her friend again. A gendarmerie made his way over to them, frowning at Tina's illegal parking. Rachel checked her face in the vanity mirror, and, with a playful wave at the police officer, they drove off.

The sun was still warm when Tina turned into the narrow lane leading to the restored Provençal villa, the white shutters offset by the honey-colored sandstone. The crunching gravel under their tires brought the Brownes' two giant black-and-tan Beaucerons bouncing toward the car, barking in excited welcome.

The house in Cassis was once part of an ancient hamlet. When Luke and Tina stumbled upon the property, they bought it because they fell in love with the view, the established olive tree plantation, and the old vines. Their immediate plan was to demolish the derelict stone structure and build something new, but Rachel convinced them to restore and renovate the ancient buildings. For almost a year, Rachel selflessly devoted her spare time to managing the restoration project, refusing any form of compensation from the Brownes. A project during which Rachel learned to cope with the many frustrating challenges of the French construction industry. In the end, Rachel certainly learned a thing or two about working with French contractors and circumventing the daunting maze of the French bureaucracy.

"I'm doing this for the love of it, you two. Accept my time as a gift and let me enjoy it," she'd argued with them. And then, for good measure, knowing Tina wouldn't yield that easily, she added, "Besides, you never know when I might need a reference for my brilliance as an architect here in France."

"Only if you treat this house as yours," Luke had insisted.

Tina parked in the shade of a huge chestnut tree and Luke appeared from the front door, dressed in leather sandals, casual khaki Bermudas and a comfortable white cotton shirt, and made his way over to them.

"Rachel, at last. We've missed you." He smiled and hugged her.

Tina herded them to the large oak table under the old plane trees in the backyard. The table was laid with a light Provençal fare of crusty bread, sun-dried tomatoes in olive oil, fresh tapenade, grilled peppers, juicy olives, and a mouth-watering assortment of local cheeses. Luke pulled the cork on a light, ice-cold rosé wine.

"Rachel, now that you're here, why don't we discuss our plans for the weekend?" Tina said with a quick wink at Luke.

Tina's smooth announcement was way too casual, and she looked up, warning bells ringing in her ears, waiting for the punch line. She knew Tina well enough that she didn't miss the subtle manipulation in her casual request. Rachel sat back in the comfortable chair and untied the clip in her hair. Soft waves of chestnut brown hair tumbled onto her shoulders and down her back. Luke handed her a glass of cold wine and she nodded her thanks.

"Right, spill it. What's bubbling in your cauldron?" she demanded.

"Not me . . . Luke." Tina shot Luke a teasing look.

Luke smiled and sat down next to his young wife, draping his arm lovingly around her shoulders. "You're probably aware of some of this, Rachel. We've had great results building our brand through last year's sponsorship of a Formula One team. So much so that I increased our sponsorship program for this year." He looked at her and shrugged before he continued. "Some of the benefits of the sponsorship include VIP tickets to key races this year. Sunday's race in Monaco is the crown event in the calendar, and we should all go."

Tina sat up, enthused, picking up from where Luke left off.

"Oh, Rachel, it's such a glamorous event, and you love fast cars. We simply must go. Luke's already arranged with Pierre for the last two executive suites in the Hôtel de Paris."

Rachel looked at the two and shook her head.

"You're so sneaky, Tina. You know very well I wouldn't have traveled all the way here for a social event."

"Yes, that I know, Rachel. But I think it's time you get out a little. How long has it been since you let your hair down—just enjoy an evening out?"

"I didn't bring anything formal to wear . . . " Rachel started weakly, but she knew her argument wouldn't fly. Tina's well-stocked, walk-in wardrobe was a treasure chest of silky Armani gowns, rich Gucci eveningwear, and seductive Nina Ricci dresses—all ready to be plundered. She smiled at the image of their shared wardrobe at university. Their similar bodies and fashion taste made it possible for them to stretch their meager student allowances a lot farther than the other girls on campus.

Ever since they met at Cambridge, Rachel and Tina had been inseparable. After university, Tina moved to London to complete her apprenticeship at the international law firm of Dunkirk and Hobbs, specializing in security law. Her insatiable appetite for hard work, willingness to spend half her life flying all over the world, and her phenomenal intellect paid off. She made junior partner in four years.

It was during those years that Tina met Luke Browne. Luke had started Browne Investment Banking ten years earlier, but was facing the real danger of losing his company, and his reputation, in a case brought before the Financial Services Authority.

Tina was a natural choice for the handpicked team Dunkirk and Hobbs appointed for Luke's defense, and for the next eight months, Tina fought like a tigress to rescue Luke's honor and livelihood. It was during this period that their mutual respect turned into something greater. They were married a year later on the white sands of Luke's holiday villa in St Barth's.

Tina clasped her hands in excitement and announced with glee, "Do I have the perfect outfits for you—impulse buys I've never worn. A black number in which you will look absolute drop-dead gorgeous—and, wait for it—a stunning silver gown for the gala evening."

"It's going to feel like the good old days when I ransacked your wardrobe," Rachel relented, and raised her glass in jest to Tina.

Chapter Three

Twenty miles east, near the hilltop village of Le Castellet, in the nearby appellation of the world-famous Bandol wine region, the magnificent estate of the renowned Chateau Léon overlooked the fertile valley below. The estate had been established in 1785 by the marauding count Maximilian Léon. For seven generations the Léon family estate had produced some of the world's most awarding Mourvedre wines.

Alain Léon, the latest in the Léon line of men, sat at his walnut Louis XV desk, absent-mindedly tapping the burgundy-colored envelope in his sun-browned hand against his chin. His dark, almost black eyes darted over the complicated set of figures flickering on the computer screen in front of him. The small scar on his upper lip, barely noticeable in the fading light, contributed to a devil-may-care element, an almost buccaneer air, that lingered about him.

The rich, wood-paneled walls were decorated with only two oil paintings, illuminated with dim, twin antique wall lights. The paintings were small but exquisite—one a Provence landscape by Cezanne and the other a self-portrait by Rodin.

The tapping of the envelope stopped mid-air, and his eyes narrowed under the straight line of his dark brows. Figures changed on the screen, seemingly in chaotic patterns, and his sharp brain made the complex calculations. With a wicked smile playing on his lips, Alain waited for the exact moment before he hit the enter key and then sat back with an appreciative sigh.

Almost seven thousand miles away, in the luxurious executive meeting room of a Hong Kong five-star hotel, an excited junior executive quietly left his desk and hurried over to whisper in his diminutive boss's left ear. A slow smile broke over the Chinese businessman's face, his wide-set teeth glistening dully in his mouth. His successful bid on the international wine auction made him wriggle with pleasure and he giggled, almost girlish.

Back in Provence, Alain stood from his chair and, and like a majestic lion, stretched his lengthy, athletic frame with a soft groan of pleasure. Broad, muscular shoulders accentuated his narrow hips and hard, flat stomach. He turned and punched a pre-programmed number on his desk telephone.

"It's done." His voice was low and clear. "Can you arrange for shipping tomorrow?"

Alain killed the connection, and like the Chinese businessman in Hong Kong, a slow smile spread over his face. Unlike the Chinese businessman, Alain had reason to be happy. He had just netted close to half a million dollars in a single transaction on the wine he'd sold at the international auction.

With a deft flip of the silver letter opener, he opened the burgundy-colored envelope and studied the heavily embossed invitation. He was faced with choosing between two options.

On the one hand was an invitation to attend the weekend festivities planned around the glamorous Monaco Formula One Grand Prix at the luxurious Hôtel de Paris. The invitation held promises of a thrilling weekend that opened with the exclusive sponsors' event on Saturday, where attendees could meet the drivers. On Sunday, the spectacle of the race could be enjoyed from the hotel's garden terrace. Finally, the famous gala dinner on Sunday evening brought the festivities to a close.

"Black tie, formal wear, and all that jazz . . . " he muttered to himself, but then reluctantly acquiesced to the reality that his attendance was required in light of his business relationships with the sponsors and hotel groups present at the event.

His other, more enjoyable option would be to spend the weekend in the relaxed company of his closest friends, watching the Formula One Grand Prix from his luxurious yacht moored in the Monaco marina.

"Much more fun . . . " he muttered again.

Alain pondered his options, not liking what he was facing. So he made a decision. "Both. I'll do both." And with that he buzzed his trusty assistant.

"Genevieve, please RSVP to the Hôtel de Paris that I will attend the Monaco weekend. And then, can you arrange to have *Vintage* moved to her berth in Monaco before Friday?"

Alain killed the connection and nodded his head. "That's better," he said and strode from the office in his long, relaxed gate.

Chapter Four

Despite her original aversion to the weekend plans, Rachel experienced a growing excitement as they made their way toward the small principality of Monaco. She leaned back in the sumptuous, soft leather seat while Luke navigated his powerful Bentley through the twisting corners of the famous Moyenne Corniche road toward Monaco, past the ancient village of Eze, stuck precariously against the high rock cliffs.

Two fun-filled days in glamorous Monaco awaited her, and, deep in thought, Rachel pinched her lower lip between her thumb and index finger. The anticipation was strangely liberating. Time to relax, enjoy life, maybe even flirt a little, and she smiled at the oddity of her rebellious deliberation. But this weekend marked the starting point of a new chapter in her life. A life where she would make time to socialize, a life where she could meet new friends. And men.

As they slowed and entered the principality, Tina leaned back and rolled her eyes at Rachel when Luke gave them a quick recital of the two-day event they were about to enjoy. Rachel smiled back at Tina, but her interest was piqued, and she listened to Luke with more attention.

"This is undoubtedly the most prestigious event on the Formula One racing calendar," he continued. "It takes almost six weeks to build the race track through the narrow, twisting streets of Monaco."

Luke parked at the Hôtel de Paris, and handing the keys to the valet, he continued, "And it is said that a driver would gladly give up any two other race wins to be crowned the winner here."

"And tonight we will meet the drivers at the sponsors' event," Tina added, joining in Luke's enthusiasm.

*

It was Saturday evening, the night before the group of brave drivers would risk their lives hurtling their machines along the twisting streets of the principality. The sponsors' event, hosted in the glamorous setting of the Hôtel de Paris, offered a short list of exclusive guests the unrivaled opportunity to meet this group of drivers.

Rachel stood on the balcony of the Empire Ballroom, taking in the view of the yacht harbor below, packed with luxurious yachts. The sun went down in a fireball of red light, dipping behind the Cap Ferrat peninsula, just visible on the horizon. With a pleasant sigh, she turned and made her way back to the table where Tina and Luke were in deep conversation with a young man.

"Ah, Rachel." Luke stood. "Let me introduce you to our star driver, Dominique Sanches."

Rachel took in the lean shape of the young man standing in front of her. He appeared too young to be risking his life piloting a multi-million dollar racing car at high speeds through sweeping corners, but then she noticed the determined look in his eyes as he took her hand.

"You're a brave man, Dominique, doing what you do."

He smiled, and in his accented English replied, "Like I tell to Tina, in the race I cannot think about the danger. I must focus on the car, the track. If I think mistake, I make mistake . . . "

Dominique continued his discussion on the team's prospects for tomorrow's race, explaining the many factors that could influence the results. It was a brief insight into a fascinating world, and as Rachel grasped the complexities of the many variables the young driver and his team had to consider, she began to understand what motivated this brave, intelligent young man.

"Now I must leave you, unfortunately," Dominique said, glancing at the expensive watch on his wrist. "It's time for me to get a good night's rest before tomorrow."

"How fascinating," Rachel commented as Dominique made his way to the exit, still locked in deep discussion with Luke.

Her eyes fell on the tall, handsome man entering the room. With an assertive stride he walked to the bar counter and gave the bartender his order. Dressed in a light blue button-down cotton shirt and a navy blue linen suit, he struck an arresting figure. His broad shoulders filled his jacket, and by the looks of his bronzed skin, Rachel suspected he enjoyed a significant amount of time outdoors. From his casual and relaxed demeanor it was clear that he was perfectly at ease in this company. A few people recognized him and nodded to him or stopped for a brief handshake. He conducted a fleeting conversation with one of the other corporate sponsors whom Luke had introduced earlier.

Then she frowned with a little stab of disappointment when a shapely goddess dressed in a low-cut, daring, red silk gown sidled up to the attractive stranger's side. Judging by her body language, she was ready to devour him. With sudden irritation, Rachel folded her napkin neatly and placed it back on the table.

"I see you've noticed him," Tina said, and Rachel dropped her gaze, a little embarrassed at being caught staring at the handsome stranger.

"Who are you talking about?" she challenged, unable to hide the defensive tone in her voice.

Tina's eyes flicked to the bar. "The sexy hunk with the dark hair you've been ogling."

Rachel felt a sudden, hot rush of blood in her neck.

"Oh, him," and glancing toward the red dress at his side, Rachel continued with a detectable bite in her voice, "He should pay more attention to his choice of companions. She might take his arm off if he's not careful."

Tina smiled and looked into her glass as she chased the olive around with her swivel stick.

"Do you know him?" Rachel asked, faking indifference.

"No, but I recognize him from last year's wine auction at Beaune—think he owns one of the largest wine estates in Provence." Then Tina smiled brightly at Rachel and said, "But you can find out more about him yourself—I think he is placed at our table tonight."

Rachel raised an eyebrow, her interest piqued, and, gathering her wits, casually lifted her gaze toward the bar counter again.

Light shock ran down her spine. He had been watching her intently. He must have managed to extract himself from the talons of the red dress, for he was now by himself, sipping his drink. His dark, brooding eyes had locked onto hers from thirty feet away, and the impact left her gasping.

Rachel turned her gaze to Tina and stuttered, "Um . . . where did Luke go?"

Tina smiled knowingly and turned, glancing over her left shoulder to where Luke was making small talk with another group two tables away. He saw Tina and beckoned her to join him.

"Got to go now . . . duty calls." Tina inclined her head toward Luke and stood to join him, her tangerine, mid-thigh silk dress drawing appreciative stares from several men across the room. With confidence, she made her way to Luke, ignoring the attentive eyes following her progress.

Chapter Five

Alain approached the cocktail bar and ordered a single malt whiskey. He nodded to the bartender, and taking his drink in his left hand, he turned to observe the room over the rim of his glass. He swirled the heavy glass and breathed in the smoky aroma of the pale gold liquor.

For the second time tonight, he noticed the beautiful, tall woman where she sat at his table, deep in conversation with her friend. He watched with interest as she laughed at a comment from someone in their party, her elbows cupped in her hands, leaning lightly on the table. Her black, silk garment revealed just enough of her legs and hugged her sensual shape, hinting at hidden treasures that any man would love to discover. She had an almost aristocratic air, accentuated by her hair pinned high with an exquisite diamond broach. He noted the sensual lines of her high cheekbones and the alluring pout of her bottom lip. A single, loose coil of chestnut brown hair dangled tantalizingly against her neck. She was simply ravishing. He sipped his drink and caught himself admiring the lines of her long legs again.

"Bonsoir, Alain," Monica greeted Alain and sidled up to his side, making sure her newly enlarged bosom touched Alain's upper arm before she laid an excessively jeweled hand possessively on his. "At last I get you alone," she whispered in a husky voice.

Alain looked down at the perfectly manicured hand and flinched as the long, fire-engine red polymer nail extensions squeezed his hand lightly. Ever since he had bought the neglected vineyard from her husband two years ago, Monica had made no secret of her intentions to bed Alain. Was it her artificially enhanced body or her promiscuity he disliked most?

"Good to see you, Monica. Now, you have to excuse me—I have someone I must meet. Oh, and your husband is anxious to find you," he said and extracted himself from her clawing hands. Monica's eyes flashed anger before she stomped off.

"Time for action—let's meet this gorgeous brunette," Alain muttered as he locked eyes with her across the room. He placed his glass on the bar counter and headed toward his table.

*

Self-conscious and a little ruffled, Rachel busied herself and opened her evening clutch, just to snap it close again. She could still feel his dark eyes on her, and her stomach fluttered as she looked up to see him approaching their table. Alarmed she turned her gaze in the other direction. "Don't be silly, Rachel. You're a grown woman, not a college student at a frat party," she muttered with light annoyance. She straightened her back and ran her hand to smooth her hair.

"Good evening." His voice was deep and clear, with just a hint of an accent. "We seem to share a table," he continued with a slight inclination of his head. "I'm Alain." He extended his hand, palm up. She hesitated for a second and then placed a slender hand in his, palm down.

"Rachel," she responded, and held her breath as he lowered his head to briefly touch his lips to the back of her hand.

So French—so charming, she thought.

"May I sit?" he asked with assertiveness, and she wondered how anyone could refuse him. It sounded more like a statement, yet he waited politely for her response. She nodded, not trusting her voice.

"Rachel . . . a beautiful name, but you're not from around here. Do I detect an English accent in the single word you've spoken so far?" A soft tease sparkled in his eyes.

She sat back in her seat and studied the beautiful creature next to her. There was a certain cavalier look about him, but that might have been because of the small scar on his upper lip. His dark eyes sparkled when he smiled, but she sensed that they could just as easy turn hard if you dared to cross this powerful man. She took in his strong, angular face. His long, black hair was neatly styled, but an unruly twist hung carelessly over his high forehead. She clenched her fists at the inexplicable urge to reach out and push it from his forehead. She noticed the long fingers and the sensual strength in his hands as he moved the drink at her elbow. Swallowing hard, she tried to recall the last time she enjoyed the touch of a man's hands on her skin.

That could hardly have happened in the last three years, she reminded herself. But even before that, Stuart had lost interest in any physical intimacy after she fell pregnant. This man, however . . . this man awakened feelings in her she had not experienced before.

Could it be because it has been so long since I . . . She shut her eyes for a moment, hoping to regain control—aware of a sudden, almost uncontrollable desire, awakening in her. The unfamiliar emotion was not what she expected when she'd decided on a short escape from her grueling routine. Then again, to be carefree for just this one night . . . to be someone else—

What harm in some innocent conversation—even a little flirting? she thought with false bravado. She opened her eyes and looked at Alain in silence, and then made an impulsive decision.

"You're quite right, Alain, I'm from London."

"So, what brings you here—to sunny Provence?"

She inclined her head toward Luke and Tina at the other table. "My friend suffers anxiety attacks if I don't visit whilst they are at their house in Cassis." In mock frustration, she shook her head and continued, "So, what's a girl to do? I'm obliged to enjoy the splendor of Provence every so often."

"How lucky for your friend, and how dreadful for you—all these sacrifices you have to make," Alain replied with a teasing smile playing on his lips, and Rachel warmed to his dry wit.

Very attractive, the way he smiles like that, she caught herself thinking. She wet her lips, swallowed, and clasped her hands in her lap. She forced herself to relax.

"You must be from around here though. I noticed you're known to a number of people here tonight." Alain studied her over the rim of his glass and she noticed the silent pleasure in his eyes at her last comment.

"And when will you return to London?"

"I fly back on Monday," and shifted in her seat. Her pulse quickened with apprehension at the direction their conversation was drifting. Painful memories of her rejection by Stuart, his disappearance into Africa, and the shame she'd felt at being forced to sell their house, flashed through her mind.

Not now, please, she almost prayed.

She couldn't bring herself to share that dreadful period in her life. Not with this beautiful stranger. Not tonight. Not here.

Her mind raced like a startled deer, eager to find a new topic—anything—to steer their conversation away from her past. "S-so . . . what do you find so exciting about a car race in Monaco—is it the glamour?"

His gaze had drifted toward her neck—distracted. Aware of the curl of hair that had escaped and twirled against the nape of her neck, she ran a hand to brush the lock away.

"Hmm, I guess you can't ignore the glamour—but so much has changed," he replied, and cleared his throat. "I remember coming here as a kid with my father—less glamorous then. It was more about hard racing—driver against driver. Today the sport has evolved, and teams depend so much on rich sponsorships to survive."

"So, you're a sponsor, like Luke?" she continued, relieved at the new direction their conversation was headed, and the tight knot between her shoulders relaxed. *He wasn't going to probe.*

A soft chuckle escaped Alain. "No, not at all. Part of my business is to buy and sell wines internationally. We also invest in young wines, and then supply hotels and restaurants with the product when it peaks." He waved a hand to indicate the room, his eyes sweeping over the crowd, before he continued, "Hôtel de Paris is one of our oldest clients, and so . . . "

"We?"

"My father and I."

"And your English—it's almost without accent?"

"English nanny," and then, as an afterthought, he added, "and the curse of my profession."

"How come?" She raised her brow, intrigued.

"Well, my father wanted me to learn from the top wine-making regions in the world—both old and new wines. I spent four years of my life learning from wine masters in Italy, Argentina, and Australia. To learn from them, I had to speak their language."

"Bet you had fun too," she replied with a teasing smile.

"It wasn't always hard work," Alain admitted with a boyish grin, his dark gaze dancing playfully over her face. His smiled stalled and his eyes drifted to her mouth.

Suddenly aware of his lingering gaze, she lowered her eyes. Hot blood rushed to her cheeks and she nervously licked her lips.

"Thirsty?" he asked with a tantalizing smile.

She nodded, and, glancing briefly over his shoulder, he summoned a server and ordered champagne.

How apt, champagne and a man that makes my head spin.

Alain sat back in his chair and raised his brows. "And that smile?"

"My secret." She crinkled her nose mischievously.

The server delivered their champagne in a silver ice bucket and Alain acknowledged it with a nod. There was a brief silence while he filled their glasses.

"Argentina always fascinated me. What was it like?" Rachel asked.

"They're a passionate people, and love their dancing."

"Sounds like you did more than studying wine then."

He nodded with a smile. "I love to dance, and wanted to learn the Tango."

"And, did you?"

"Sure, the traditional way. First though, I had to learn how to dance the woman's part. Only when I had mastered that, was I allowed to lead."

"That's not true—you're just making that up."

"Believe me, that's the truth. 'Imagine a jungle cat stalking its prey,' my instructor taught me."

A warm tingle ran down her spine.

"Do you like to dance?" His smile was inviting.

"Sure." she nodded, and silently thanked her mother for the hours she had to endure in dancing school.

"Then we have a date—tomorrow night at the gala?"

"Yes, but no stalking, please."

The red dress was lurking at the bar counter, glaring at them with venom in her eyes. "On that note, your companion is looking for you," she said with a taunting glint in her eyes, and Alain followed her gaze.

"It's getting crowded in here. Let's go for a walk." Alain stood, extending his hand. On impulse she stood, placed her hand in the crook of his arm, and walked from the room with Alain.

Chapter Six

A pleasant evening breeze cooled the air to drive away some of the afternoon's heat. They stepped through the slow revolving doors and a soft sigh escaped Rachel as she inhaled the fresh, cool air. The angry barks of powerful engines had been put to rest in their pit garages for the evening, and from the nearby yacht harbor came the pleasant sound of halyards clanging against metal masts in the breeze.

They turned toward the sea where the early evening sky was still tinted in a lingering, deep mauve, and slowly meandered in the direction of the Monaco yacht basin. Alain draped his jacket over his shoulder and she realized that he, like her, was happy to leave the stuffy, crowded atmosphere of the ballroom.

"Better," he said, rather than asked. He lifted his gaze and stared out onto the ocean as they continued their slow walk to the harbor. A small frown played on Rachel's face and she briefly pondered her decision to leave the ballroom with this man—a virtual stranger. Oddly, she felt completely safe and quietly at peace walking beside him in the last light of the day. She glanced sideways at his lean, muscular frame, broad shoulders, and long legs, and then flipped her hair back with a determined look on her face.

What's wrong with a bit of innocent fun?

They continued their conversation, switching between music, politics, and other topics with ease. When Rachel briefly mentioned her love for museums, Alain impressed her with his knowledge of nineteenth-century art. She was delighted to learn they shared a deep respect and admiration for the work of artists Degas and Rodin. His voice filled with passion when he described particular aspects of their techniques, and she was left with a strong impression that he might be a proud collector of their work. But she didn't inquire, reluctant to interrupt the enjoyment of watching him talk, taking in his beautiful face and hands. His dark, almost black eyes shone bright with intelligence and passion, a ready laugh always waiting to escape.

They came to a low concrete railing overlooking the yacht basin. The air was filled with the sounds of joyful laughter and soft music from the gleaming yachts below. Alain raised his hand to return a wave from a blond giant on a sleek super-yacht lying to his left, the name *Vintage* displayed in discrete transom lettering. The giant beckoned toward them.

"You know him?"

Alain nodded. "I should. He's my best friend. More like my brother, I guess."

She looked down at the scene below them. The elegant yacht must have been at least a hundred and fifty feet long. The deck was bathed in soft light from the luxurious interior, where about a dozen people were enjoying drinks and canapés.

Alain turned to her as she was taking in the scene on the yacht. "Let's join them?"

"And crash their party?" She searched his face for signs of levity. Surely he couldn't be serious?

"Not at all. They're expecting me—but unfortunately my attendance at the sponsors' event was unavoidable." He shrugged his broad shoulders once. "Business."

She bit her lower lip as she considered his invitation.

"You don't have to stay long . . . I will walk you back if you're uncomfortable," he said, glancing back over his shoulder at the impressive façade of the Hôtel de Paris, now dressed in bright lights.

"Just for a while then." She flipped open her phone to call Tina.

Alain waited for her to finish her call and then walked to an entrance gate, swiped his access card over the reader, and pushed the spring-loaded gate open for her.

As they approached the sleek, dark blue hull of the sailing

yacht, Rachel saw she had underestimated the size of the vessel. Two slanted masts disappeared in the dark evening sky high above them. The spacious teak deck was uncluttered and wide, with several people milling around, enjoying the relaxed hospitality.

They were met at the ship's gangway by the tall blond man, his long, curly, sun-bleached hair tied back in an unruly ponytail. He flashed Rachel the most brilliant, white smile.

"Rachel, meet my friend Marque. Marque—Rachel," Alain introduced them with casual ease. Rachel acknowledged Marque's warm smile and stepped out of her platform sandals before boarding the yacht. She looked up in mild surprise at Alain's lengthy frame.

He's at least six inches taller than me. At five feet, eight inches, Rachel preferred the company of tall men.

Marque reached out to help her on board and she noticed the dry, steel-hard hand of someone who filled his days with physical activities. A fellow yachtsman, she thought.

Intelligent, gray eyes, playful and ready to smile, met hers as he greeted her in a soft, relaxed voice. "Well, well, well. Now I see why you've left us for the Empire ballroom, Alain. *Enchanté* Rachel, *enchanté.*"

"Nice to meet you, Marque." His casual demeanor was infectious. "I like your yacht."

Marque chuckled and shook his head. "Thanks, Rachel, but I sail a *real* yacht," he replied, smiling at Alain.

She raised her eyebrows at Alain, trying to fathom the meaning of Marque's words.

"*Vintage* is mine, but Marque despises her—not enough of a true racing yacht." Then, laying a familiar hand on Marque's shoulder, Alain continued in a melodramatic voice, "His one and only true love is called *Pure Joy*, and she lies at anchor in St. Tropez, where she eagerly awaits the return of her master, ready to take on the challenge of the next regatta." For his remark, Alain received a playful punch from Marque on his shoulder.

"Let's get a drink," Alain suggested and turned, laying a light hand onto her lower back. She inhaled at the pleasure of his touch as he guided her toward the luxurious interior. Soft background music played from the hidden speakers of the entertainment center. Acutely aware of Alain's warm presence at her side, they made their way inside.

"Your yacht?" she said, lifting her eyebrows to take in the polished mahogany woodwork, the gleaming stainless steel winches, and expensive electronics.

"I enjoy the ocean. It relaxes me." He nodded toward the people mingling on the deck. "And I often use it for business. Come, let me show you around."

Rachel accepted his invitation and Alain took her on a short tour of *Vintage*. With evident enthusiasm, he explained the yacht's features, reaching up with his long, muscular arms to point to the tops of the masts, or stroking an instrument lovingly with his strong, sensual hands. Rachel followed close on his footsteps, reveling in the deep, reassuring sound of his voice, hearing, but not necessarily listening—enjoying herself.

Alain came to a halt and she bumped into him, grabbing at his steely biceps for balance. Her hand lingered on his upper arm with a will of its own. She blushed and dropped her hand.

"And this is the master stateroom." Alain's voice turned low and husky.

Aware of his eyes on her, she glanced around the cabin, taking in the luxury of the beautiful wood paneling, the deep, piled carpeting, and the two Cezanne paintings—softly illuminated. With just a tang of excitement, her gaze drifted to the oversized, carved mahogany bed dominating the room. She noticed the fine, crisp Egyptian cotton linen, and the scattering of large, soft pillows. The air in the room turned warmer.

Alain's eyes locked onto Rachel and her heart started racing, thumping wildly in her chest. He took one step toward her.

"Anyone object if I kiss you now?" His voice was hoarse. Rachel had to part her lips to breathe, the air suddenly thin, and her heart fluttered like a trapped wild bird in her chest at the closeness of his magnificent body. A warm tightening started swelling deep inside her.

He gently stroked her cheek with the back of his hand and she inhaled sharply at the electricity of his sensual touch on her skin. She cleared her throat and stepped back. The edge of the bed touched the back of her legs. With slight alarm she realized she was trapped; but then, strangely, the thought thrilled her—the thought of being vulnerable to his power.

"Anyone?" he demanded in a low voice, and she craved the warm, manly odor of his body as he leaned closer into her.

"No . . . nobody," Rachel answered, amazed at her own bravado, her voice a soft whisper. A strong arm encircled her, and leaning farther into her, Alain pushed her back, lowering her slowly onto the bed, his lips brushing briefly against her face. Nervous, Rachel placed her hands on his muscular upper arms, feeling the trembling strength dancing under her fingers. She sank back into the luxury of the bed and the feathery touch of Alain's lips stroked her neck, slowly moving toward her ear. A hot thrill of pleasure raked her body as he nibbled her earlobe, kissing his way to her mouth.

Their lips touched. Alain tugged sharply on the tender flesh of her lower lip, and then caressed it with his tongue. With another sharp tug he whispered, his voice hoarse, "I've been wanting to do this all evening . . . your mouth is so beautiful, so inviting . . . "

Rachel groaned a soft reply. "Alain, please . . . "

With urgent passion, Alain claimed her mouth and lowered his upper body, his chest weighing down gently onto her breasts. Her nipples hardened in response.

Something deep inside stirred. A low arousal, a lust, woke in her, growing, eager and hungry. Surrendering, she opened her mouth, moaning softly as she invited Alain's tongue to explore. She met the hard, powerful thrust of his lower body against her pelvis, grinding herself into him.

A deep groan rumbled in Alain's chest, his breathing coming faster as the warmth of his arousal pressed against her body.

"Alain! Where're you guys? The fireworks are about to start!" Marque's voice boomed from the deck above.

Shock splashed over Rachel like cold water and her eyes shot wide open. With a deep moan, Alain tore himself away. Rachel sat upright on the bed, passion thundering wildly through her body. She raised her chin and straightened her hair, avoiding Alain's eyes on her.

Alain stood, and extending his hand, he helped her up. "Best we join them—they might think I'm holding you captive down here." She smiled, suddenly self-conscious, but collected herself, and stood to make her way back to the deck.

*

Alain followed right behind Rachel, watching the sensuous sway of her slender hips as she stepped up onto the deck to join the rest of the party in watching the fireworks. A strange, deep desire rushed over him. He tilted his head and frowned in the darkness, struggling to rationalize the strange, new feeling with logic.

The urge to kiss her—where did that come from?

He was no stranger to lust, but this was something different—almost tender. He simply couldn't stop himself—this had never happened to him before. The sweet taste of her mouth, the delicious smell of magnolia on her silky skin, the soft moan from her throat—all lingered in his mind. He frowned, puzzled. Then he turned to study Rachel's upturned face where she stood next to him, her gaze on the spectacular explosions high in the sky.

"I think I've taken enough of your time," Rachel's spoke, her eyes still on the fireworks above them. Then she turned to face him. "Time to leave you so you can tend to your guests."

Alain smiled down at her and made a swift decision. "I'll walk you back now, but you must agree to see me tomorrow. Can you join us on my yacht for the race?"

"No, I can't—my friends will be expecting me," but he noted the disappointment in her reply.

"Then I will see you at the gala dinner," he insisted, and Rachel nodded in agreement.

Chapter Seven

Tina was perched on the edge of her seat, her body turned to take in every expression on Rachel's face. Her eyes darted with excitement while she listened to Rachel recount the events of the previous evening with Alain. Breakfast had been a lengthy, torturous affair, but finally, they were alone and free to speak in private.

"And that's all you know about him—he owns a yacht, and trades in wine?"

"We talked about other things too," Rachel defended weakly. "Besides, I didn't want to get into my horrible history with Stuart."

"But you obviously had a good time," Tina probed, her unrelenting eyes searching Rachel's face.

"Yes, I had a great evening, thanks." She tried to brush over the details, but the lingering smile remained on Tina's face. Almost ten years as best friends would do that. She simply couldn't hide anything from Tina.

"And?" Tina left it hanging.

"Well, you know . . . we went to his yacht, met some of his friends. A couple of drinks, and—"

"And?" Tina persisted.

Rachel exhaled and nodded. "And yes, we kissed."

"I knew it," Tina exclaimed, clasping a hand over her wide smile in excitement. "Where?"

"On his yacht," she responded, capitulating without much further resistance. "Alain showed me around, and we ended up in the stateroom."

Tina nodded, eager to hear the rest.

"It was like nothing I've ever experienced before, Tina," she continued. She ran a hand down her arm, from her shoulder to her wrist, and continued in a softer tone, "Look, I still get goose bumps just thinking about it."

"Yes, and about time you had some fun too—and thank heavens he seems to know how to kiss a woman."

A soft glow came to her cheeks. "Yes, he certainly knows how to kiss. But it's more than that. I don't know if I'm ready for this . . . " Her voice trailed off.

"Nonsense," Tina replied with vigor. "You've been hiding from men for too long. Just enjoy it—no strings attached."

"But that's just the problem, Tina."

"What do you mean?"

"I think it is more than just fun for me. I could easily fall in love with him."

"He should be so lucky," Tina tried to keep it light, but Rachel noted the dark concern that clouded her friend's eyes. Ever since Stuart deserted her, Tina's been rather protective.

After disappearing from her life, Stuart vanished in the vastness of Africa. His assignments took him to the remotest of places on that wild continent, and her letters and emails went unanswered.

A year had passed before Rachel finally decided to file for divorce. But Stuart's disappearance had made the process tedious—and expensive. It had been more than three years since that dreadful day when Stuart had abandoned them—and almost four months since the last communication with him. Letters from Rachel's lawyer were returned, unopened and undelivered. Email messages unread.

The sudden sharp bark of a high performance engine screaming from the pit garages announced the true purpose of the weekend's activities and shattered any further attempt to continue their conversation. With a little shriek of shock, Rachel and Tina hurriedly donned the foam earplugs Luke had provided to them earlier and focused their attention on the drama that was about to unfold in front of them. From their seats in the hotel's garden terrace marquee, they enjoyed a close-up view of the track, and

Rachel reeled at the crushing noise levels of the cars sweeping past them on the warm-up lap. She stared at Tina in disbelief and mouthed to her friend in the deafening din, "This is insane . . . "

A frantic tension rippled through the crowd as throngs of excited fans, clad in the bright team colors of their heroes, eagerly took their seats in the stands. Nervous technicians scurried around, making their final adjustments in desperate attempts to satisfy the demands of the tense drivers seated in the body-hugging cockpits of their racing machines.

The instant the set of five red lights went out to start the race, the earsplitting noise of twenty-two racing machines exploded from the starting line. The noise reduced somewhat while the cars raced their way around the back of the track on the undulating, twisting streets. Then, like approaching thunder, the noise levels grew steadily stronger again, to explode with an insane crescendo when the cars flashed through the corner directly below their seats.

The noise and raw power of the brightly colored cars flashing past them was overwhelming. Luke joined them and Rachel turned to watch his lips as he relayed some critical information about his driver's progress, but most of his words were swept away when another car screamed past them.

She abandoned her effort to understand what Luke was trying to communicate, sat back in her seat and started twirling a long lock of hair around her finger. She turned her gaze toward the harbor where she could clearly make out the tall, twin masts of *Vintage*. Her mind drifted to the events of the previous evening, and a soft smile lingered on her lips at the pleasant memory of the time spent with Alain.

"Alain." She whispered the name, enjoying the sound of it. She frowned at the memory of her impulsive acceptance of his suggestion to go for a walk. As if that hadn't been rash enough, she then joined him on his yacht—a man she hardly knew.

Yes, what was that, Rachel? she thought, but enjoyed the warm glow brought on by the memory of the evening's events. Thinking back, she could not recall ever being so impulsive . . . so swept away by passion. She touched her lips at the memory of their fiery kiss on the yacht, and then warmth rushed to her cheeks when she recalled Marque's untimely interruption.

The guests on his yacht must have included some of Alain's closest and most trusted friends, but his relationship with Marque was different—deeper. The two men had been friends since kids, but something must have happened in their past — something that forged a strong bond between them — maybe a life-changing event.

A light quiver ran through her body as she recalled the wild passion of Alain's embrace. She sat back with a deep sigh at the memory of his soft touch on her cheek, the gentle caress of his lips on her neck, their bodies melting together on the bed. Her hand lingered for a moment on her mouth, and she smiled at the thought of Alain's sharp tug on her lip, urging her to let his tongue explore her mouth.

"Probably a good thing we got interrupted," she murmured.

She hugged herself at the memory of Alain's light linen jacket draped over her shoulders when they walked back. She'd felt safe within the warm, silky folds of the inner lining, relishing its manly smell.

At the hotel, he waited politely for her while she collected her room key, and then rode the elevator with her to her floor. It felt good being with him—so strong and self-assured, yet compassionate and gentle—so different from Stuart. Alain was the type of man she'd always wanted in her life. A man who understood himself—a man with passion. A man who would stand by his beliefs.

She shifted in her seat at recalling the disappointment of Alain bidding her a polite goodnight at her door. One kiss—that was all they had. She wanted more. More of the sensual sensation, now that the passion deep inside her had been stirred.

She lifted her gaze to the masts again and mumbled softly, "I'm sure there must be another woman," and then more vehemently, "or women!" Alain's lean, muscular body, good looks, and wealth left her with no doubt that he would have a long list of beautiful women in his life. She found herself wishing she had probed him on whether he was currently in any serious relationship. Suddenly agitated, she muttered, "You've just met the man, Rachel."

She had a deep desire to see him again and regretted her decision not to join Alain and his friends on the yacht for the race. With a slight pang of guilt, she turned to face Tina on the seat next to her. "I love you," she mouthed through the noise, and received a quick hug from her.

A loud crash and the sudden, deep inhale from the crowd made her glance up at the giant flat-screen monitor directly opposite the terrace. The slow-motion caption replayed the images of a dark blue, mangled wreck shooting from the tunnel into the bright sunlight, skidding out of control, to crash into a barrier. Two French TV commentators were frantically announcing the gravity of the crash. With relief, she watched the driver struggle from the wreck, but then inhaled with shock at recognizing Dominique when he removed his helmet and walked off to a safety marshal. He waved briefly to the crowd before he disappeared, and Rachel collapsed back in her seat and exhaled loudly.

Someone's going to get killed. When will this madness ever end?

Chapter Eight

The Formula One Gala Dinner, an event of exclusivity and splendor, made for one of the social highlights on the Monaco calendar. It didn't surprise Rachel to see the names of Prince Albert and his beautiful new South African wife on the list of attendees.

Rachel stepped into the lavish ballroom dressed in a figure-hugging, silver couture gown. The classic design hinted at her cleavage and the low, draping back revealed her shoulders, drawing several appreciative looks from the men around the room. With a slight nod, she acknowledged the knowing look in Tina's eyes.

She smiled at the battle of wits she'd had with her friend in finally selecting her gown for the evening. For almost an hour she modeled the seemingly endless selection of evening gowns from Tina's expansive walk-in wardrobe.

"Too daring—I might as well go naked," Rachel complained all too often.

"Oh, come on, Rachel—you have the body for it. Flaunt it. Some debonair Frenchmen will appreciate it," Tina would counter. In the end, the combination of chilled champagne and Tina's persistence won the battle.

And Tina was right. Despite her hectic schedule, she had always found the time for her morning run. It didn't take her long to regain her tight body after the birth of her children, and the gown's fit accentuated the curves of her taut figure. It had been a while since she had found the time or the inclination to dress so sensually.

Tina flipped her hair over her shoulder with confidence and flashed Luke a radiant smile as he escorted them to their table. She was dressed in a daring, strapless, couture gown, the soft mint green stunning against her sultry skin.

Seconds after they were seated, Rachel became aware of Alain's intent eyes on her from the far corner of the room. Her heart jumped at the sight of his tall, muscular frame. He was dressed in a tailored black dinner jacket, his bronzed face contrasting with the pristine white of his formal shirt. He smiled and struck out across the room toward their table with long, easy strides.

"You look lovely tonight, Rachel," he said with a husky note in his voice. Rachel smiled up at Alain, and then turned to Tina and Luke.

"Alain, this is my dear friend Tina and her husband, Luke."

Alain greeted them with a warm smile.

"Please, sit," Luke invited, and Alain took a seat at next to Rachel. "Was your driver hurt?" he directed at Luke.

"Just his confidence. But the mental challenge to come back in the next race will be tough on him," Luke replied, and Rachel reveled at the ease with which Alain found a common connection to get the conversation started.

As they settled into the rhythm of light conversation, Rachel noticed the effect of Alain's charismatic personality on Tina and Luke. Light laugher soon rang from their table, and when Alain excused himself to see to his guests, it was with a sense of shared disappointment from all at their table.

"My guests must think I have deserted them, but I will be back to call on you for our dance," Alain promised before he left. Rachel suddenly wished the servers would hurry along with the evening's dinner.

Eyes downturned, Tina sat in silence opposite her. Rachel noticed the teasing smile on her lips. "Yes, and what now?" Rachel asked.

Tina toiled with the seared scallops starter in front of her. "Alain's a fascinating man," she said, leaving the statement hanging.

Rachel sat back, inclining her head as if surprised by Tina's comment. "He sure is. What do you think, Luke?"

Luke looked up at her from his plate. "Certainly. I believe he owns a couple of exotic vintage cars. Wouldn't mind having a peek at his garage one day."

"Men . . . " Tina mouthed at Rachel and shook her head in mock amazement.

By the time the servers hauled in the elaborate cheese trolleys, the performing four-piece band had succeeded in warming up the crowd with a couple of well-executed numbers. Alain made his way over to their table and laid a light hand on her chair back.

"A man of my word." He held his hand out to her.

She stood from her chair with controlled grace, but her heart was racing. She tensed at the pleasure of his touch on her arm as he guided her to the dance floor. Strong arms encircled her body with a familiar confidence, and then they glided across the floor. She shivered with excitement. He truly was a gracious dancer and he steered them with skill and confidence through the crowd.

Pleasure rippled over her skin at the sensual touch of his warm hand on her bare back, and she relaxed, enjoying the closeness of their bodies as they moved together. She reveled at the easy balance of his muscular frame and was just beginning to lose herself in the sensual haze of music and movement when the dance ended.

"That didn't really count as a dance," he suggested and took her in his arms again when the next song started. The band had increased the tempo, and soon Alain had them sweeping across the floor in flowing, graceful arcs.

As they flitted over the dance floor, Rachel found herself distracted by the latent strength in his shoulders and upper torso, the warmth from his body. With a light frown she willed herself to concentrate on the intricate dance routine Alain had them executing.

That's better, she thought and focused on her dancing, but then, while her hand rested lightly on the nape of his back, she had difficulty restraining herself from playing with a tangle of his long hair tickling her fingers.

Get a grip on yourself, Rachel.

Her heart raced to a healthy rush as the pace of their dancing increased, and she started breathing deeper, matching the slow, strong rhythm of Alain's breathing. He was fit and strong, and she enjoyed the closeness of his male strength as they swirled across the parquet flooring.

The band started another slow, romantic song, and he pulled her tighter to his body. She gasped at the intimate closeness of their bodies. Her hand trembled, but she slid it higher up on his back. Inhaling his manly warmth, she closed her eyes and rested her head against his shoulder. His hand traced down her spine and she sighed softly.

Song after song, they enjoyed the thrill of dancing, their bodies locked in rhythm to the pulse of the music, oblivious to their surroundings.

I've never desired a man more—does he feel the same?

Time stood still.

The band stopped, and Alain led Rachel to a table on the balcony to enjoy the cool, fresh air. He leaned forward to say something, but then looked up with mild surprise when a server approached their table with an apprehensive request to clear the table.

Surprised, she glanced at her watch. Alain's mouth drew in a tight line of disappointment, but he stood from the table. He extended his hand to her. "Let's go."

Chapter Nine

The elaborate ballroom was quiet and almost deserted as they walked out. At the door, Rachel turned for Alain to drape her shawl. His hand briefly stroked her bare shoulder, and she caught her breath at the electric sensation of his touch.

"I'll walk you to your room," Alain said, his voice husky.

The ride up in the small, brightly lit elevator was awkward. It came to a jerky halt on her level and she stepped out with some relief into the dim lighting of the passage. Her throat tightened at the close presence of Alain at her side as they walked down the wide hallway, their footsteps muffled by the thick carpet.

They reached her room and she tried to hide the quiver in her hands as she slotted the electronic key into the door. Alain stood, close to her, his breathing stroking the fine hair in the nape of her neck. The door clicked open with a soft buzz, and she turned to face him. His closeness made her shiver involuntary. She swallowed, unable to speak. She didn't want the evening to end yet—she didn't want to say good night.

He reached over her shoulder, and with one hand, he pushed the door open. Without saying a word, they stepped inside. The door shut by itself and Alain stepped forward and took her in his arms. He cupped her face in his hand, willing her to look deep into his eyes.

"Alain . . . " But then he kissed her tenderly and her resistance faltered. Her whole body ached and urged her to accept this, but her mind raced to find the words to stop this assault on her senses.

Alain slipped the shawl from her shoulders, stroking the skin of her bare back. Strong fingers trailed down the curves of her body and she pushed herself against his deep chest at the pleasure of it.

She closed her eyes and lost herself in his clean, muscular

aroma—the warmth radiating from his strong body. Her starved body took control, craving more of the pleasurable sensations—sensations she had not enjoyed for years. Too late, she realized she couldn't turn back from this path. With strange objectivity, ignoring the alarm bells clanging in her ears, Rachel surrendered, her body accepting the pleasure of his touch.

Oh, please, I can't stop this—don't want to stop this, she thought, knowing her feeble struggle was faltering, weakened by the passion growing deep inside her.

Alain slipped his jacket from his shoulders, and, lifting her without effort, he carried her to the bed. Their lips still locked, he lowered her onto the bed. Her breathing became rushed, and little gasps escaped her lips every time his hands touched her bare flesh.

With skillful hands he unclipped her gown and slid it from her shoulders, exposing her breasts. Strong fingers slowly traced her naked skin, and Rachel closed her eyes, lost in the exquisite sensation of her skin coming alive to his touch. Then, ever so gently, Alain cupped her breast, his hand gently squeezing. She moaned aloud as his hot breath stroked her bare breast, the warmth so close to her hardened nipple. Tender lips touched her exposed nipple, and she arched her body, moaning with deep pleasure, her head tilted back.

With practiced hands, he lifted her hips and slipped her gown from underneath her. She heard his sharp inhale at the sight of her near-nakedness as he stared down at her. Lust burned in his eyes.

With urgent fingers, she started ripping at the buttons of Alain's shirt, exposing his golden skin, warm to her touch. She raked her nails lightly down the hard, contoured shape of his chest, leaving long trails of reddened skin. Goose bumps lit up like wildfire on his shoulders.

The need to have him close to her overwhelmed her, and she reached for his shoulders, drawing him closer to her. Alain lowered himself next to her, supporting his weight on one elbow, and she started at his warm arousal, hard and urgent, against her thigh. A strong hand traced the curve of her breast, then down her quivering ribs, to pause briefly on her hips. Gently he parted her legs with his hand. His fingers traced the delicate lace patterns of her thong. She closed her eyes, and, reaching for Alain, she urged him closer. He shifted onto her, sliding his hips firmly between her legs. She arched her body at the pleasure of his hard arousal against her. Her eyes fluttered and she raised her head, seeking his lips. She moaned as their lips touched. Their tongues tangled and her arousal spiked.

Alain nipped her bottom lip once. Then he nibbled softly at the sensitive flesh in her neck, working his way down to her breasts. With sudden realization at what would come, Rachel held her breath, waiting. His lowered his head to her scantily covered womanhood, his tongue tracing the embroidered flowers of white lace. Her pelvis arched in response. With some impatience, he removed her thong and lowered his face to her curly mound of hair.

Her breathing shuddered, almost sobbed with anticipation, and she grabbed a fistful of his thick, black hair—not to stop him, but to hold his lovely head there. She sensed him, his warm breath whispering on her most tender flesh, pausing, teasing, the anticipation driving her mad. He spread her thighs wider and she inhaled sharply, her taut body shivering in want. He lowered his head and then, as his lips touched the warm moistness between her legs, the air exploded from her chest.

With a slow, growing urgency, his tongue stroked her, and she started floating, drifting on a soft cloud at the pleasure of it. She moaned deeply, grinding her pelvis upwards, wanting more, seeking that glorious tongue in her.

Alain's hand slid upwards, his palm hard on her flat stomach, pausing momentarily on her heaving ribs before he captured her left breast, caressing it until she rolled her shoulder in ecstasy to his touch. He took a nipple firmly between his thumb and forefinger and squeezed softly and she inhaled sharply with pleasure.

With delicate fingers he opened her swollen, ready lips further, exposing her to the full wickedness of his clever tongue, darting and flicking into her until a soft, agonized cry escaped her heaving body. She thrashed her arms on the pillows beside her, and then bundled a fistful of the white cotton sheets in her hands, drowning slowly in the magic of his touch. Her back arched in spasm and her naked body slithered and twisted on the bed.

Suddenly his finger slid into her, stroking her, raising her to a new level of almost unbearable pleasure. She gasped aloud when he took her full, pulsating arousal into his hot mouth, sucking hard and urgent. His tongue stroked her, urging her on, until her aroused womanhood throbbed with a pulsating life of its own, tightening on his finger inside her. A deep warmth flooded her body as Alain coaxed the desire captured inside to burst out and take flight. Her hands clawed at the taut muscles in his shoulders, and then the tide took her, lifting her higher—unstoppable. Without warning the wave spilled over Rachel, crushing the air from her chest and her body exploded in orgasm.

"Alain, Alain!" she cried out while spasms rippled through her body, the rush of ecstasy so intense tears welled in her eyes. Waves of pleasure washed repeatedly over her and momentarily shut down her other senses—no sound, no sight. She thrashed her head from side to side, in absolute silence, biting down on her lip; and then slowly, almost painfully, the wave receded, leaving her trembling and sated on the bed, gasping for air.

With patience, Alain waited in silence until she was ready. Then he came onto all fours, raw lust burning hot in his dark eyes, his own erection rock hard in readiness for entering her body. Tantalizing, teasing her further, he ran his wicked tongue along her flat stomach toward her navel. Then, abruptly, he froze, a dark frown on his forehead. With his right hand, he touched the fine scar on her stomach, inspecting it with intense attention in the soft light.

"This is from a cesarean," he said, rather than asked, his voice gruff.

"Yes," Rachel answered hesitantly, confused by the sudden change in his behavior. Alain jerked upright from the bed.

"You have a child," he stated in measured words and stepped back.

"T-two." She cringed, frightened by the dark shock on his face.

"One question." His palms were raised in front of him as if fending off an attack. He swallowed visibly. "No *buts, ifs,* or *ands.* Just a straight answer." His voice grumbled like low thunder, a warning to do exactly as he commanded.

She nodded agreement in silence and clasped her hand over her mouth in shock. What is *happening* here?

Alain glared at her, breathing heavily as she waited on his question. "Are you married?" His dark question resonated in measured words.

"Yes, but—"

"No *buts,* I said!" he shouted at her, his eyes now flashing black in anger. Or was it disgust? Alain glared at her for a second, fire flashing in his dark eyes. With uncontrolled anger, he flung a pillow across the room, toppling the large vase of roses on the stand. Glass shards sprayed in all directions while water ran slowly from the stand and dripped onto the carpet.

Then he turned, a bunched fist to his forehead, and stood in silence for a second. With a grunt, he snatched his shirt from the floor and snapped it on violently. He grabbed his dinner jacket and stormed from her room without looking back. The door closed behind him with a final thud.

Rachel flinched when the door slammed close behind Alain. Uncontrollable shivers ran through her body and she was chilled to the bone. Dazed, she took in the room, barely noticing the long-stemmed white roses lying scattered in the pooled water on the stand or the shards of glass covering the floor. Hurt and angry, she flung another pillow across the room.

"You presumptuous bastard!" she yelled in helpless frustration, adrenalin rushing through her veins. "How arrogant you are—no *buts, ifs,* or *ands.* What do you know about my life?"

She had been separated from Stuart for more than three years.

Three years of no intimacy, no contact and no financial support.

"I'm raising two kids on my own whilst rebuilding my career, you insensitive oaf."

Just as suddenly the anger left her. She slumped back onto the bed like a rag doll. He'd discarded her like a cheap toy. The familiar emptiness of rejection overwhelmed her, and she rolled onto her side and curled her long legs under her chin in a fetal position. The duvet was still warm from the heat of their bodies, where minutes ago they were locked in intimacy.

She shut her eyes, but knew sleep would avoid her for the rest of the night.

Chapter Ten

In the far distance, over the Mediterranean Sea, the eastern sky was painted in a light, pre-dawn mauve as day eagerly awaited the sun's majestic ascent. Soon the bright, golden light of the sun would burn off the wisps of mist hanging low over the calm waters of the Monaco yacht basin.

For more than an hour, Rachel sat in the window seat, motionless. Her knees pulled tight into her chest and her body stiff from not moving, she stared vacantly at the scene unfolding in front of her through reddened eyes. The cup of coffee at her feet sat cold and forgotten.

Predictably, sleep had avoided her for most of the evening, her only companion being the raw, wounded feeling in her chest—a painful reminder of the events that had played out on the luxury bed behind her.

She shook her head in quiet disbelief, trying once again, to process the hurt inside her. That dreadful drop into a deep, dark pit that came with rejection was all too familiar. The thought was drilled through her heart like a crude spear, once again at the hand of a man she'd allowed too close to her.

His violent behavior from last night circled like dark demons in the room, ready to assault her fragile mind the moment she dropped her defenses. Although she had replayed his cruel behavior over and over in her head, she still couldn't find a way to dull the pain it caused—the pain of total rejection.

Once again, a man had chosen to turn his back on her. And once again she'd allowed herself to be exposed to that hurt. The deep wound of disappointment brought on by Stuart's departure three years ago was slashed wide open again.

A shudder ran down her body at the thought of the many nights she lay awake in bed, hurt and afraid. No, terrified. Terrified of not being a good parent, terrified of not being able to pay the rent, terrified of being alone.

Suddenly a cold anger rose in her. The past hours of pain and sadness turned to a white-hot heat as she pushed the feelings of rejection away.

"Who do you think you are, you pompous hypocrite?" she shouted at the ceiling, her fists balled in frustration. With a vicious swipe of her hand, she flung the coffee cup crashing against the wall. Brown liquid ran in ugly stains down the luxurious wallpaper.

Filled with anger and a sudden urge to act, Rachel stormed into the bathroom, eager to wash the tears from her face and the pain from her heart. She showered in haste and quickly applied some make-up. Her anger suddenly had a focus point, and the words began to form in her mind. She wanted to hurt him. Hurt him where he was most vulnerable. She needed to do this—tell him exactly what a cold bastard he was.

"Alain, the so-called strong one—the all-powerful, almighty Alain. You're a judgmental, arrogant, hypocrite," she rambled in anger and snatched a dress from the hanger.

With those thoughts of vengeance she closed the door behind her and made her way to the concierge in the lobby, determined that Alain would know her last thoughts about him. She would leave them in a handwritten message that he could carry with him—to remind him.

*

Alain woke early, ordered coffee, had a quick shower, and, without care, tossed his evening clothes into his black leather valise. He dressed in a white, open-neck shirt and comfortable navy linen trousers. Pushing his feet into his soft leather driving shoes, he placed a quick call to the concierge to have his car ready.

Not in the mood for breakfast, Alain wasted no time checking out. He turned to leave through the revolving doors when Rachel stepped from the elevators. She hesitated when she noticed him, but Alain gripped his valise with firm determination and headed for the door. Without acknowledging her, he walked straight past her.

The valet attendant placed his valise in the trunk and Alain jumped into his low-slung, Seychelles blue sports car. The classic DB6 was in pristine condition and was Alain's favorite vehicle from his collection, but at that moment, the pleasure of owning the car was wasted on him. Without as much as a glance, Alain engaged first gear and roared away.

He drove fast but controlled, taking the most direct route via Boulevard Princess Charlotte to the A8 West. Within minutes, he entered through the tollgates and settled in for the drive back to the estate.

His mind racing, Alain tried to collect his thoughts. The picture of Rachel exiting the elevators would not leave him. Dressed in a pleated white chiffon dress that showed her lean figure, she looked hurt and almost afraid when she stepped from the door.

Irritated, he tried to clear the image of her big eyes from his mind. He had noticed the hesitant hand, raised as if to address him, but she faltered when he stormed past her. He clenched his jaw determinedly.

"Time to forget about her and move on, Alain," he muttered and pushed a hand through his hair.

Ever since returning to Chateau Léon, Alain had had no shortage of female company. Unmarried at thirty-four and the heir to one of France's most elite wine estates, Alain was an eligible catch and on the mailing list for almost every social event in Europe. His athletic frame, sulky eyes and black mane of waving hair had earned him the unwarranted reputation of a heartbreaker, but he had always been very discrete in his interactions with the many beautiful women who crossed his path.

There were times, during his stay in Argentina as a hot-blooded, aspirant wine maker, when he might have been a little promiscuous, but he was young and carefree then.

Once there was someone special—a woman who mattered. She made him consider the idea of taking their relationship to the next level. They experimented with the idea, moved in together, and lived like committed, loving partners. After four months, they woke one morning, and, over coffee, engaged in a frank discussion about the merits of continuing their relationship. They parted as friends with the knowledge that passionate lovers don't necessarily make good life partners. After that, Alain's interests in woman became less important as he spent more time focusing on their family business, concerned with his father's health.

His phone flashed, and, with a curl of his lip, he inserted the earpiece and accepted the call.

"Bonjour," he barked.

"Alain, Marque here. You're still going to make it, aren't you?"

The question left Alain silent. The episode with Rachel had distracted him, and he had forgotten completely about his commitment. Marque was expecting him on his yacht for the St. Tropez *Regatta des Bravades*.

The two men were close friends and had been sailing competitively since they were young boys. All that sailing experience eventually paid off, and they'd finished a respectable fourth at last year's Rolex Swan Cup.

"Don't tell me you forgot." Marque's irritated disappointment was tangible over the roar of the engine.

Alain's eyes narrowed and he clenched his jaw. He was in no mood to be chastened. Then he relaxed his tight grip on the steering wheel. Without his participation, Marque would be short-handed and couldn't be competitive in the race. They'd spent months preparing the yacht, and had drilled the team to perfection. He simply couldn't get out of this one.

"My gear still in the locker?" he asked, knowing the answer.

"Yes, as always."

"See you in an hour," he replied, and killed the connection. Shifting the powerful engine into a lower gear, he roared up the steep incline.

*

St. Tropez arguably could be described as one of the prettiest harbors in the Mediterranean, its long, curving promenade allowing tourists to steal glances at the sleek yachts moored in the turquoise waters. On the day of the regatta, the participating yachts were moored along the quay, offering both spectators and competitors a close-up view of the hardware.

As last year's winner, Marque's forty-five-foot Swan was honored with the central spot in the harbor, and when Alain arrived, she was lying proudly at anchor, gleaming in pristine white. Alain boarded the sleek yacht, stepping directly onto the teak to avoid making any scuff marks.

"Aha, my executive officer is on board," Marque announced with visible relief, and in typical European fashion he greeted his friend with a kiss to each cheek. "We have less than an hour before we cast off, so hurry up," he added, encouraging Alain with a friendly slap on the shoulder.

Six hours later, the grueling sailing in the strong winds and wild sea behind them, Marque sat, his back resting against the gleaming polished mahogany of the bulkhead, his long, sun-browned legs stretched out in front of him on the blue-and-white-striped upholstery.

Alain seated himself across from Marque, propped his bare feet on the seat, and took in the gleeful, grinning face of his friend. It was tinged a shade darker by the sun and wind of the day's sailing. In silence, they stared at the simple glass trophy on the drop leaf teak table between them, a testament to their hard work of the last twelve months. Joyous laughter and excited shrieks from the deck above mixed with the clink of ice cubes and the low beat of jazz over the stereo.

"Thanks, Alain. I couldn't have done it without you," Marque said in a brief moment of seriousness.

Alain shook his head. "Sure you could."

Marque shrugged in response and drank deeply from his ice-cold beer, studying Alain's face all the time. "So who is she?" he asked, taking care to place the tall, frosted glass on the coaster in front of him.

Alain shifted in his seat. "What do you mean?"

"Come on, Alain, you've been just a little distracted ever since you returned from Monaco. Something, or someone, has your attention. My guess is it's a woman. Is it Rachel?"

Alain sat, pensively staring at the flashing amber colors of the single malt he was swirling in the heavy crystal glass. The same color as Rachel's eyes, he thought wryly. A deep frown formed on his forehead. He'd never been able to hide anything from Marque. He raised his glass to Marque and took a sip. "Yes, it's Rachel."

Marque was silent, waiting for him to continue.

"I don't understand what it is, but since the moment I saw her, she's affected me in a different way. Don't get me wrong—I want to bed her—but I also can't get her from my mind." He looked into Marque's questioning eyes and continued, "We made an instant connection. I was drawn to her like no other woman before. She's beautiful and intelligent—"

"But . . . " Marque let it hang in the air.

Alain sat back and pushed the glass away from him. "Just one small problem—she's married with two kids."

"Married?" Marque asked incredibly. "Well, I didn't see that one coming." Marque sat back, leaned his head back against the bulkhead, and studied Alain's face. Then a slow smile spread over his face. "She got to you, didn't she?" he said with a slow, confirming nod.

"Much good it does me." He stood abruptly, eager to leave. "I've got to go."

Chapter Eleven

"Thanks, Leena. Same time tomorrow then?" The nanny turned to leave and Rachel locked the door behind her. She rested her head against the coolness of the doorsill and stood for a moment, exhaling slowly. With effort, she pushed herself away, made her way to the soft, wide sofa, and flopped down with a heavy sigh. With extended fingers, she gently massaged the dull headache throbbing at her temple. "Just a minute's silence, please—just a minute." She closed her eyes and relaxed her shoulders, shedding the day's pressure like a heavy coat.

With a deep sigh, she opened her eyes and retrieved a large envelope from her leather briefcase. Her hand started to tremble, as she once again read the return address on the back. She flipped the envelope and studied the embossed crest, proudly displaying the emblem of the family-owned Chateau Léon. A cold tingle ran down her neck. This letter could change her life if it bore the good news she was hoping for. She shuddered involuntary at the alternative.

For weeks, she had worked on drafting their firm's bid on the contract for the restoration of the grand chateau in southern France. Once one of the finest examples of the French revival architectural style, the chateau was badly damaged in a fire in 1984. Now the owner, Eugene Léon, wished to commission a reputable architectural firm to oversee the project and restore the chateau to its former beauty. It was a lucrative project, and her throat closed at the thought of being awarded the work. It would leapfrog their firm from fragile startup to success. The news contained in the envelope was so important that Rachel had waited until she reached the safety of her own home before she could bring herself to open it. So many things would be different if this envelope bore the right message. So much would change back at the office space she shared with her partner in the funky West End of central London.

A soft smile touched her lips as she remembered the day when Peter noticed the wording on the brass nameplate as the contractor was fixing it to their office door. *Swift & Simon—Architects* the small bronze plaque read on the big red door.

"Swift before Simon . . . Where did you learn your alphabet, my pretty Rachel?" he asked in mocked seriousness, smiling at her over his red, horn-rimmed reading glasses.

"'Ladies before gentlemen,' that's what my parents always taught me, my dear Peter," she responded, laughing over her shoulder and stepped through the entrance to their offices. Peter, who'd stood by her during her dark hours of doubt and loneliness. In Peter's company she was safe to speak her mind freely. During those months, it was thanks to Peter and his partner Gary's patience and support that she managed to find balance in her life again.

Iain and Mia's shrill shrieks of excitement interrupted her thoughts, and with a soft sigh, she put the letter aside. She smiled and clapped her hands in excitement at the two kids bursting into the room. They giggled, their little bare feet pattering on the whitewashed parquet flooring as they sprinted to her waiting arms. Iain streaked ahead, long and strong for his age, his deep blue eyes bright with excitement. Mia followed, a little more sedate, wiping a wet curl of ash-blond hair from her face. Bumping and laughing, they launched themselves at Rachel on the sofa. Their warm, clean little bodies squirmed and fidgeted against her until they finally began to calm down, waiting for her to start reading.

"What shall we read tonight, then?" Two little hands pointed in unison to the worn, yellow book on top of the stack.

"Again?" she asked with mock surprise. Two heads bobbed in unison again, and opening the book with flourish, she started reading in a clear, animated voice. At the tender age of three years, the twins still loved to hear the story of Peter Rabbit over and over again.

It was not until later, after the twins were tucked in their warm beds, that Rachel could bring herself to open the letter. She poured a glass of red wine, kicked off her shoes, and sank down on the comfortable sofa, tucking her legs under her. Without further hesitation, she ran the silver letter opener along the top of the envelope, and, ignoring the business card dropping on her lap, she glanced over the content.

"*. . . and it is my pleasure to inform you that our decision is to award this project to your firm, Swift & Simon.*"

Rachel dropped her hands in her lap, and as she tilted her head toward the ceiling, warm tears filled her eyes. A soft relief flooded over her, and the tight knot between her shoulders relaxed. A nervous giggle escaped her, and she reread the entire letter again.

"Thank you," she whispered once, and then joyous laughter filled the room.

"Peter—got to tell Peter," she exclaimed, and with a little shriek of happiness, she leaped from the sofa and ran to the kitchen phone.

"Peter, we got it!" she blurted out, and, before he could say a word, "The Léon project is ours!"

For a moment the line went silent.

"Peter, you there?"

"Yes, of course. Are you sure . . . I mean, when did you hear?"

"I just opened the letter. Sorry Peter, I just couldn't do it at the office."

"Wow, Rachel darling—this is big. Big with a capital B!" Peter's excitement increased as the news sank in. "We will have to think about expanding our little business now, won't we?"

Rachel nodded enthusiastically at his comment. The excitement and relief made her giddy, and for a second she frowned with some guilt while pouring her second glass of wine. Then she raised her glass and consoled herself with the promise to run an extra two miles in the morning.

"We will have to look at our workload for the next year. You might have to relocate to Provence, Rachel. Will you be able to handle that?" The rational side of Peter started surfacing after the initial flurry of excitement.

Rachel popped an olive in her mouth and chewed on it, deep in thought. Then she sat up straight with sudden purpose, her eyes wide. "I can handle it. I will rent something close to the chateau and get a nanny for the twins during the day. Eugene sounds like a reasonable man, and I will structure the work around my schedule." Then, with more excitement, "Oh, Peter, I can hardly believe it's happened. We worked so hard for this, and now, we have it."

For the next forty minutes Rachel and Peter's excited conversation darted from project logistics to resources and staffing, and then finally drifted to scheduling for the project.

Later, with the promise to clear her calendar for an early meeting in the morning, Rachel hung up. The light buzz in her ears wouldn't stop, but despite her exhaustion, she smiled happily. Three years of hard work had finally paid off.

Taking her glass, she walked to her bathroom and started to run a long, hot bath. She undressed and glanced at her image in the mirror. Not bad, she thought. A mother of two children, at twenty-nine she still had a remarkable body. Rachel always enjoyed individual sports at school—triathlons and sailing Laser sailboats. The years of cycling, swimming, and running had shaped her body to be lean and lithe. She no longer competed in triathlons, but the discipline to train regularly had stayed with her. Her morning runs were important to her, mentally and physically.

She untied her hair, letting it tumble to her shoulders. She tilted her head and she studied the image of her naked body with a critical eye. Her gaze came to rest on her strong, well-formed shoulders.

"Too bony," she mumbled.

Her gaze moved to take in the slender shape of her toned arms. "Hmmm, desperately need some sun," she continued her critique.

Then, with a slight wrinkle on her forehead, she turned her

focus to her waistline. Turning sideways, standing on her toes as steam started clouding the mirror, she carefully inspected the sensuous curvature of her flat stomach and hips for any unwelcome evidence of her weakness for chocolate. She traced her index finger down her chest, across her stomach, to finally hover, hesitating just above the hairline scar, barely noticeable, below her navel. She touched the scar lightly and smiled at the memory of the day the twins were born. The day that forever changed her life.

A dark thought suddenly crossed Rachel's mind. Alain.

"That man," she said with disgust.

For months she had buried any thoughts about him deep away, but as her hand touched the hairline scar, the hurtful memories of that night, more than six months ago, rushed back. Annoyed at herself for allowing any thought of him back in her mind, Rachel grabbed her robe and snapped it on with a sharp pull on the belt.

"Don't let him spoil the day," she said aloud and lifted her chin. Then she rested her hand lightly on the area below her navel and whispered, "Today has changed everything, my little babies."

Rachel arrived at her office early the next day, two large coffees in hand. Peter studied her over his funky red reading glasses with a quizzical expression on his face. Then he pushed the design he was working on to one side, and smiled warmly.

"You're early."

"It's the start of a new day, and we have a lot to discuss."

The rest of the morning was spent in Peter's office while they worked on drafting the rough terms of the contract for the project. Just before lunch, a knock on the door interrupted them. It was Rachel's assistant, Darcie.

"Rachel, I have Monsieur Léon on the line for you." Rachel inclined her head at Peter and then stepped out to take the call in her office.

"Monsieur Léon, bonjour." She sat back in the comfort of her chair and opened her notebook. "I'm not fluent in French yet. I hope you will forgive me if I tell you that I'm studying the language and making progress—slowly," she announced in French, grimaced and crossed her fingers. Her attempt at the language sounded so terrible. She paused, and as she realized he was waiting for her to finish, she continued in English, "I also want to thank you for your trust in our company. We're ecstatic that you chose us, and look forward to working with you on this project."

Monsieur Léon chuckled softly and replied in a warm voice, "Please call me Eugene, and if you don't mind, I'll call you Rachel. If we're going to work together for the next year, we might as well be on first-name terms. And don't worry about the French—I'm fully bilingual. In fact, an added bonus for you might be that I can help you with your French. What do you say?"

"*D'accord*," she replied with a smile.

Warming to her client's warm demeanor, Rachel relaxed as they started discussing the preliminaries of the work. But despite his gentle approach, Eugene had absolute clarity about the final outcome of the project. He articulated his goals with remarkable accuracy, and when Rachel pointed out some constraints they might have to consider, it was evident he had already studied them as well as their collective impacts.

"So what are the next steps, Rachel?" Eugene asked, curious to understand the timeline.

"Well, assuming we can get the legalities out of the way quickly, I plan to move into a house in Cassis to be closer to the project," she informed Eugene.

When Tina and Luke heard of her plans to rent a cottage in Provence, they insisted Rachel use their house in Cassis. They had always felt indebted to Rachel for the months she selflessly dedicated to the renovation of the derelict hamlet they bought just outside Cassis. This gave them an opportunity to reciprocate. They insisted and wouldn't accept any excuses from Rachel. In the end she relented, and accepted their offer graciously. Rachel also knew she wouldn't be able to do it without Arianne, their trusted housekeeper. Not only was Arianne a lifesaver, but was also an excellent au pair and much loved by the kids.

"Hmm, Cassis . . . "

And Rachel knew he had checked the references she had provided.

"Yes, I fell in love with the area when I did some work there . . . " she replied in a neutral voice.

"I've seen the work you did on that hamlet renovation in Cassis. Your sympathetic touch for preserving the salient aspects of the architecture was what convinced me to use your firm. I'm glad you will be the one on the ground here."

Sly old fox, Rachel thought. "Well, I'll be living there while I'm working on our project. The hamlet belongs to my close friends and they insisted I use it."

After her meeting with Eugene, Rachel sat back in her leather chair. Deep in thought, she tapped the pencil on her blotter. Her gaze drifted toward the London skyline to come to rest on the slow revolving London Eye, barely visible through the drab, foggy mist.

Her life was about to change. For the second time in a year, she was making her way down to the south of France. On her previous visit to that country, she came away hurt and wounded. This time her visit would ring in a happier period of her life, she vowed. After all, she thought with just a bit of sarcasm, one bad experience, and now one good experience. That leveled the score.

Chapter Twelve

The next day, Rachel arrived at the office later than usual. That's the price you pay for working too late, she thought and sat down behind her desk. She pushed back in her chair, enjoying the comfort of the soft leather against her skin, and brought the cup to her nose, inhaling the rich aroma of the hot coffee. The muted sounds of ringing phones and expensive CAD/CAM equipment buzzing busily in the background bore testimony to the team of Swift & Simon's staff, hard at work on one of the many architecture projects awarded to their firm.

She glanced with pride at the activities on the other side of her office's thick glass panels, a soft satisfactory smile on her lips. Her career had finally taken flight again. She was happy again—happy for the first time in a long time. Her professional life was on track, and the fledgling business she and Peter started three years ago was finally beginning to pay off. The culture they had created of treating their clients as the single most important aspect of their business was showing results. The steady growth in business over the last eighteen months had made it possible for them to build a small but successful architecture firm right in the heart of London. Even after all these months, each morning as she stepped into their offices, her chest would swell with warm pride as she was greeted by the small group of happy people working together.

But it was the Léon project that made her heart pump faster. News of Swift & Simon winning the work had reached the streets, and a couple of the more established architecture firms in the city were quick to indicate a willingness to partner with Swift & Simon on future work. It was especially sweet for Peter, for they had won the contract from under the noses of MSC, his previous employer and the most prestigious architecture firm in London. The increased workload of the Léon project took up every spare minute of her day, but despite the long hours, she often caught herself smiling as she pondered a design or calculated important load-bearing points.

Then there is my personal life, she thought. She shifted in her chair. Not enjoying the coffee anymore, she pushed the cup aside, a small frown on her brow.

That side of her life would soon change for the better—especially with the news she'd received from her lawyer last week. The court date for the obligatory appearance was set for the week before she left for France.

Divorced—finally.

She mouthed the strange word, experimenting, remembering the mixed feelings that rushed through her mind when she first heard those words from her lawyer. At first, all she experienced was relief—relief it was finally over. Then came sadness. She and Stuart had created two beautiful children. But he didn't see it that way. And she should have been more vigilant to the early warning signs.

Stuart first pursued a career as a professional tennis player, but a nasty back injury put an end to that. While Rachel worked hard at establishing her career as a new, young architect, he struggled to find direction after his injury, eventually setting his sights on photography. She achieved early success in her career, but he struggled in the tough world of professional photography.

Then Stuart lost both his parents when an Air France aircraft plunged into the Atlantic Ocean, hours after taking off from Brazil, killing all 216 passengers onboard. Ignoring her instincts and overwhelmed by sympathy, she married Stuart three months later on a hot, September afternoon.

She married out of sympathy. Sympathy—it felt almost alien to think that such an emotion could drive her into the arms of a man. How bizarre. Imagine feeling sympathy for someone like Alain.

"Alain," she whispered his name. Rachel bit her lower lip in thought. She had tried her best to remove all memories of Alain from her mind. For months now, she had wrestled down any thoughts of Alain and banned them from her head. But they kept on coming back.

At first she tried to reason that it was purely her physical attraction to him. After all, the man had a lovely physique. A godlike face and an Olympian's body—how unfair. The physical enjoyment and pleasure she enjoyed at his strong, gentle hands—the deep, hidden needs he coaxed from her body with his wicked, clever tongue—all those passions she could understand and explain to herself. It was all just physical. *Three years of celibacy will do that to you*, she thought wryly.

She was a young, healthy woman. Her body craved intimacy. But brushing that aside, she couldn't deny the emotional connection they'd made and the immense pleasure she experienced in his company.

His wit—his intelligence. The love for art they shared. The long, easy conversations they'd had, and she smiled at the memory of one of the many fascinating discussions they shared during their brief relationship.

A feeling of deep loss spilled over her at the memory of how safe and protected Alain made her feel in those two short days. And she missed that so much in her life. Then the dark, painful memory of their last night together caused her to swallow hard.

Should I let him know about my divorce? Maybe that would change things?

No, he acted like a lunatic—there is no excuse for that kind of behavior. "What a Neanderthal." Rachel voiced the angry words and clenched her jaw. How could any man do that to her? How dare he cast her aside like an old, broken toy, presumptuously assuming she's immoral.

"Good riddance, Rach —" She jumped at the phone ringing at

her desk, interrupting her thoughts. Then, glancing at her watch, she smiled at the realization that her conference call with Eugene Léon was about to start.

"Bonjour, Eugene. *Comment ça va?* How is my favorite client today?" she sang into the speakerphone and flipped open her laptop, switching smartly to the electronic file containing the latest progress report.

"Oh, Rachel, you make an old man's heart jump."

In the span of an hour, Rachel stepped Eugene methodically through the three draft proposals they had prepared for his consideration. Eugene would have to decide on one of the schematic designs, and once agreed, the Swift & Simon team would shift into gear to create the blueprint designs. But Eugene wanted absolute clarity before making his decision, and he had several pertinent questions on the various aspects of the designs.

"I will give you my final answer by Monday," he stated when their meeting finally started winding down. "When were you planning to be down here?"

"I'm moving into the house next Wednesday, Eugene—lock, stock, and barrel."

"I will come over to welcome you personally," he declared before ringing off.

Chapter Thirteen

It was late autumn and the sun was heading toward a fiery dip in the Mediterranean when Rachel finally drove up to the house in Cassis and parked under a huge, bare oak tree. Arianne opened the door and rushed down the wide stone steps to welcome them. Mia and Iain struggled impatiently with their safety belts, eager to get out of the car and be reunited with Arianne.

Later that afternoon, Eugene's vehicle came to a halt outside the house. Rachel stepped out and welcomed him.

"Eugene! Thanks for coming over." She reached out to him and he kissed both her cheeks.

"I wanted to make sure my architect has settled in and was not in need of anything." He laughed and lifted a case of wine from the trunk. "A good year, and something you will not find in any wine store," he declared with a wink and carried the wooden crate to the front door.

"As long as it doesn't constitute a bribe," she joked back. "Come, let's enjoy some refreshments."

"I can't stay," Eugene answered in response to Rachel's invitation, "Just wanted to thank you for making this sacrifice to move here for the project."

"Hardly a sacrifice, Eugene." Rachel smiled, indicating the lovely setting and the beautifully restored house behind her. "But thank you for checking in."

"So, when would you like to visit Chateau Léon?"

"Tomorrow morning . . . if that works for you?" Rachel suggested, keen to experience the chateau first hand. Thus far, all they had to work on were the photos Eugene had provided and the official surveyor drawings.

"You're sure? You just arrived. Don't you need a bit more time to unpack and settle in?"

Rachel laughed. "No, I'm fine. Thanks, Eugene. I travel light and besides, I have Arianne to help me."

When Eugene departed later, it was with the promise to collect Rachel at nine o'clock the next morning. "It's difficult to find the first time, so I will happily drive you there tomorrow."

*

Rachel had spent many hours studying the photos Eugene provided—imagining the splendor of the chateau, gauging the impressiveness—but she was not prepared for the majestic impression the building made on her as Eugene drove them along the neglected, bumpy gravel road leading up to the chateau. Century-old plane trees lined the approach to the chateau, a silent welcome from ancient guards.

Her face reflected in the car window, eyes wide with excitement, as she leaned forward to glance up at the aged stone walls. She marveled at the sight, her eyes bright with excitement and awe. Despite the ravaging damage caused by the fire, the stately building stood proudly in the surroundings of ancient oak trees and the backdrop of pristine vineyards. The new estate complex, constructed after the fire, could be seen on a hill in the far distance.

They walked up the wide marble staircase to the front door and Rachel hardly noticed the other vehicles parked in the forecourt.

"There you can see where we repaired the roof after the fire," Eugene started when they entered the impressive building through the heavy wooden front door. Then he shrugged, showing his French side, and continued, "Well, of course, it doesn't look that great, but it was good enough to protect the building against the elements."

Four men from a removal company were busy crating a few pieces of large furniture while workers were sweeping the floor to clean the building in preparation for the work ahead. In the far corner, she noticed the tall, masculine shape of someone dressed in designer blue jeans and a black turtleneck cashmere sweater. He had his back to them and Rachel took in the wide shoulders and the sensual slant of his muscular back tapering down to his narrow hips.

Something about the casual stance of his lengthy, athletic frame was strangely familiar, but at that instant, she couldn't place it.

"Come, let me introduce you to my son, Rachel," Eugene invited, indicating the tall figure. "I don't have the energy of a young man anymore . . . he will be working with you on the project while you're on site."

As they approached, Rachel noted the ease with which the man gave his instructions to the foreman. He was clearly used to being in charge. A niggling warning flashed in the back of her mind as they approached. He turned to face them.

Shock rocked Rachel to an abrupt halt. A cold vise clamped over her chest, forcing the air from her lungs. Her mouth went dry and her vision blurred. For a second, dizziness threatened to topple her.

"Rachel, let me introduce you. This is my son, Alain Léon."

*

The sudden sight of Rachel hit him like a mule kick in the stomach. Alain flinched reflexively, clamped his jaw and, just in time, caught himself from stepping back.

He took in the lithe figure of Rachel, dressed in black wool trousers, functional black court shoes, and a white silk blouse. The second button on her blouse was undone and revealed just enough of the soft, creamy skin under the slender curve of her neck. A sudden urge to once again smell the aroma of her body welled up in him. The power of it stunned him.

Before he could prevent it, his eyes flashed to take in the

sensuous curve of her hips and the subtle protrusion of her youthful, pert breasts under the thin material of her blouse.

He returned his gaze to her face, unprepared for the shock of her beautiful eyes, flaring like warm cognac. Surprise flashed high on her cheeks, and her soft lips parted ever so slightly at the sudden intake of air. Her hair was down, cascading from her shoulders, framing the beautiful, familiar features of her face.

"Pleased to meet you." His throat was dry and he tried to avoid staring at her sensual lips. He settled for the eyes instead, but his chest tightened suddenly at the burning embers staring at him from under her long lashes.

*

"Likewise," was all Rachel could muster, her mind racing like a trapped animal, but she followed Alain's example and didn't acknowledge their earlier, disastrous encounter. She shook Alain's dry, warm hand and a light wave of electricity thrilled down her spine. The world around her suddenly appeared fuzzy—like in a dream.

How could this be happening? she thought in desperation. When Alain left her hotel room that evening in Monaco, she truly hoped to never see him again. His rude, uncouth behavior left her hurt and vulnerable. She would never be able to work with him on this project.

"Let me show you around, Rachel, so you can see the rest of the chateau for yourself," Eugene offered. His words jolted her back to reality, and she jerked her hand from Alain's firm, dry grip. Swallowing hard, not trusting her voice, she simply nodded at the welcome escape of Eugene's suggestion. Avoiding Alain's dark eyes, she turned sharply and followed Eugene from the room, aware of Alain's piercing eyes burning into her back as she walked away. Squeezing the leather strap of her handbag in a tight grip, her mind raced anxiously to find a way out of the unbearable situation she was facing.

She couldn't see herself working on this project any longer.

But Swift & Simon desperately needed this project—and the financial consequences of reneging on this contract could destroy their firm. Peter simply had to step in to replace her.

While Eugene guided Rachel through the interior of the building, she made her decision. When they finally completed the tour, she excused herself and hastened outside to make a phone call.

Her hands shook violently as she dug her phone from her handbag. She closed her eyes and took a deep breath of air. Then she flipped the phone open and hit the speed dial for her business partner.

"Peter, Alain is Eugene's son," she whispered loudly on her phone the second he answered, foregoing any formalities.

"Hold on, Rachel, what on earth are you on about?" Peter's calm answer came back.

"Alain, he is Alain Léon—he is Chateau Léon. Peter, I simply cannot run this project."

"You mean *that* Alain?" Peter's shock managed to stir Rachel into near hysterics. Trembling, she turned in a small circle as hopelessness washed over her, stamping her feet in frustration.

"Yes, *that* Alain. Peter, you have to step in—there is no other way."

The line went silent and Rachel sensed she was beginning to lose her argument. "Peter, you can understand? You know the history." Her voice was almost pleading.

Peter cleared his throat, and, dejected, Rachel dropped her head to her chest.

"Rachel, you know I can't do that—not even for you," Peter answered in a slow, gentle voice. A deep sigh could be heard over the line. Then he continued, "I'm spread too thin on the projects here in London already. My clients will go ballistic if I drop everything now and disappear to France."

After Monaco, she had shared the pain of that disastrous evening with Peter, and he was quick to point out how thankful she should be for not having a man like Alain in her life. But now, all that has changed. Alain had become an important part of her life—her client. With growing impatience, she listened to Peter stating his points. Easy for him to say, but I'm the one who has to face the arrogant Alain, she thought wryly.

"Listen, Rachel, he is just another idiot fool who doesn't deserve someone like you. He's a nothing. Don't let this upset you. Just treat him as another client."

As Peter continued his rational explanations, she was forced to accept the facts. They were faced with one of only two options.

The first was for her to continue managing the project. The second option could lead to significant financial losses—even the real risk of closing the doors to Swift & Simon. She could never do that to Peter—not after all he had done for her.

"Well, Rachel, have you seen enough for today?" Eugene asked with a tired smile when she rejoined them after her telephone call. With a sudden pang of guilt, she realized that it had been a long and exhausting day for Eugene. He needed to get some rest.

"Yes, thanks—for now," Rachel answered quickly, "and now I know my way here, so you don't have to chaperone me all the way from Cassis again."

"Good point." Eugene turned to Alain. "Alain, can you drive the lovely Rachel back? I'm going to relax with my novel."

Chapter Fourteen

Nerves fluttered in her stomach as Rachel followed Alain to his vehicle. He held the door for her and closed it with a solid clunk once she was seated. She sat, hands folded in her lap. Her back was stiff and straight, barely touching the seat. She stared straight ahead as Alain walked around his silver Maserati and took his position behind the steering wheel.

"Where to?" Alain asked curtly and pushed the starter button without waiting for her answer. The lively engine roared to life and settled into a menacing burble.

"A50 to Cassis, thanks. I'll direct you from there."

As Alain maneuvered the low car over the rough gravel service road, Rachel flashed a quick look in his direction. She took in the strong line of his profile, the sun-browned hands, long fingers delicately maneuvering the steering wheel. Against her best intentions, her eyes dropped to take in his long, muscular legs in the fitted designer jeans, and she squirmed in the soft leather seat at the stirring in her lower stomach.

"Rachel, we need to talk about this project." Alain spoke first, his gaze fixed straight ahead on the road.

"What about it?" she blurted, the hair in her neck tingling with warning. Now that she'd decided to go ahead with the project, she would not back down. They had won the opportunity to complete this project through hard work, but more importantly, financially Swift & Simon needed this project. She could not back down.

"I don't want you to do this work for the Léon family." Rachel flinched at his deliberate choice of words. He wanted her to know it would be a family decision. "I want you to cancel the contract with Chateau Léon. Naturally we will compensate you for all expenses and the time you've put into the project so far."

She clenched her fists. A wild rage rushed her and anger flared hot on her cheeks. She shot Alain a fierce look, her ears buzzing as blood roared to her head. "We have a professional commitment and a legal agreement with your father to complete this project. If you think I am going to walk away from this simply because you have some moral issue with me, I have news for you." She panted, flushed and out of breath.

"Don't you, of all people, dare talk to me about morals," he hissed at her, his knuckles white as he clenched the wheel, his dark eyes glaring straight ahead.

Her voice turned cold. "What are you trying to say, Alain—that you're holier than thou?" With some satisfaction she saw her words hit home when his mouth snapped in a hard line, the ropey muscles in his forearm bulging in protest as he gripped the wheel tighter. Angered and provoked, she continued in a low voice, "And don't you dare lecture me about my life. You know nothing about my life—nothing." For a brief second he glanced at her, lightning flashing in his dark eyes before he returned his attention to the road.

He breathed deeply. "Can we keep it professional and not get personal? This project will be reassigned to another firm."

"No! Remove yourself from the project, Alain Léon." Her voice was high-pitched with fear, and anger threatened to close her throat. Her body strained against the seatbelt as she twisted to face Alain and her breathing became shallow and rushed as she reasoned with him. Helplessness threatened to overwhelm her, and her hands trembled violently.

His eyes flashed briefly to her breasts, and the car swerved violently as Alain corrected the steering, narrowly missing a parked scooter on the side of the road.

Keep your eyes on the road, she thought with some satisfaction.

"I cannot remove myself. If I do, my father will step right back in. He is old and weak, and should save his energy."

She went silent and sat back in her seat, staring at the road ahead. She was not going to back off. She could not back off—they needed this project. But what would happen if Alain convinced Eugene to cancel the contract? Fear suddenly laid its familiar cold, vise-like hand on her heart and squeezed. He won't do that. The quality of our proposal outshone all the others, she reminded herself bravely. Starting the process afresh would put the project back at least another three months.

Alain drove on in silence, his face blank as he stared ahead. He shot her another glance. Her jaw quivered and she turned her face away to hide her emotions.

He cleared his throat. In a gentler voice, he said, "Okay, I'll give it a try. I will work with you on this project and put aside our history. You think we can handle this professionally?" he asked, a softer tone to his voice.

Rachel swallowed hard. "I can. Can you?"

They completed the journey in an uncomfortable silence. When Alain finally brought the vehicle to a slow stop at the front door, Rachel exhaled with relief. She stepped from the car and Iain and Mia appeared shyly at the front door.

"Hi, Mommy," Iain greeted her as he walked down the stone steps, clutching his favorite toy car under his arm. Hypnotized, his eyes glued on the low profile of the powerful vehicle parked in front of the house, he descended the steps, one by one. Without so much as giving her a hug, oblivious to her outstretched arms, Iain made his way toward the gleaming vehicle, and, resting his hand on the sleek curve of the front door, he looked up at Alain.

"What kind of car is it?" he whispered with wide eyes, his little voice shaky with total admiration.

Alain glanced toward Rachel, seeking guidance. She just smiled, lifted one shoulder, and left him to his own devices. Uncertain, Alain squatted on his heels next to the boy and smiled.

"It is a Maserati. Would you like a ride in it one day?"

"Yeah!" Iain exclaimed, a bright smile on his face. Then, turning to Rachel and tugging at her arm, his eyes pleading, he continued, "Can I, Mommy? Can I?"

Rachel smiled down at Iain next to the gleaming machine. "Sure, Iain, maybe one day," she replied, feeling guilty at lying to her son. She tried to hide it, but the poignant tone lingered in her voice.

Alain's car disappeared down the road and Mia appeared silently at her side. She placed her hand in Rachel's and looked up at her mother. "Iain likes the man, Mommy. Do you?"

I do, my baby, I do, she wanted to answer, but kept her thoughts to herself. Then, turning to enter the house with her two kids, she said softly, "But he's not for me."

Chapter Fifteen

The bumpy road leading up to the chateau was filled with potholes and in desperate need of repairs. Rachel slowed to a crawl, navigating her rental car toward the chateau. She exited her vehicle and started up the stairs to the heavy, hand-carved front door. The past two weeks she'd been working closely with Eugene on finalizing the design he selected. Once they had agreed on all the detail, Eugene would hand most of the work over to Alain.

She compressed her lips.

Alain.

Soon she would be working with him on this project. She dreaded the day, but couldn't deny the flutter of excitement in her stomach. Just the thought of seeing him again made her heart race. Irritated, she dumped the car keys in her purse and mumbled to herself, "As Peter said—he doesn't deserve me. Forget about him."

Eugene's crew had erected a makeshift table for her in the ballroom, and Rachel headed straight for it. Eager to finish the final edits to the design Eugene approved, Rachel turned all her attention to the blueprint drawings in front of her. Soon she was engrossed in her work.

"Hi, Rachel . . . "

She shrieked, jolted upright from the table and spun around. She exhaled slowly, a little embarrassed.

"Sorry, didn't mean to frighten you." He smiled at her, his teeth brilliant white against his bronzed skin.

She took in the powerful shape of his lean body under the soft cotton shirt. She frowned lightly and scowled at the warm jubilation washing over her. Why should she be so delighted to see this man?

"No, it was me—I was deep in thought," she replied with a wave of her hand.

Close on Alain's heels, two strangers marched into the room. From their appearance, Rachel deduced they were the contractors Alain had selected. Alain and Eugene had put tenders out for the restoration work and short-listed the contractors based on their experience working on relevant projects. She knew they had interviewed the contractors and made their selections. It was time to meet the crew.

"Rachel, I've requested the contractors to meet with us today so that I can introduce them to you." He turned and invited the men to join them. "This is Thierry Roux, main contractor." A short, barrel-chested man beamed a wide smile at her, his gray, friendly eyes set deep in a wrinkled face.

"And this is Alexis Du Toit, electrical contractor." Alexis nodded. His fair complexion turned a deep red and he lowered his gaze, stuffing his hands in his pockets.

"*Enchanté, Madame*," both greeted her, and Rachel was not surprised to find that neither of them spoke any English.

The front door slammed shut, and a third man sauntered into the room. Alain turned to face him. "Ah, and this is Pierre Mas, plumbing contractor—Pierre, Madame Swift."

As Pierre approached, his eyes shifted down to take in Rachel's legs, then rested for seconds on her breasts, before he lifted his gaze lazily to meet her eyes. Rachel shifted, uncomfortable. Then she lifted her head high and met his gaze with a steely look in her eyes.

"*Enchanté, Madame*," the plumber declared, and as Rachel returned to her drawing table, he glanced at the other two men and mumbled something under his breath.

His words were lost on her, but Alain tensed next to her. Electricity charged the air, and a little muscle jumped in his jaw. He stepped forward and instructed the other two contractors to leave the room. In silence he waited patiently for them to exit.

Then, with one swift movement, he planted his body in front of Pierre. The soft, measured words that rumbled from his chest reminded Rachel of an approaching lightning storm—dangerous and threatening.

"*Pourquoi?*" Pierre raised his shoulders and threw his hands in the air, challenging Alain's instructions. Alain took one menacing step closer to Pierre, his chest heaving with barely controlled rage. Towering over the man, he pointed a long finger toward the door, his forearms tightened in anger. Leaning into Pierre's face, he whispered with menace, "Leave, now."

She watched in silence as the man turned abruptly and left the room. "What was that all about?" she asked, hiding the quiver in her voice. Violence always frightened her.

"His behavior was offensive. I will not tolerate that. His replacement will report here tomorrow morning."

"I could have dealt with it," she replied bravely, yet silently relieved Alain had taken care of the situation. Alain's eyebrows snapped into a dark line, and he shook his head.

"Forget about it." Then he stepped toward the table to inspect the final additions to the plan. He leaned closer and Rachel could make out that familiar, slightly woodsy smell of his roused maleness. In a long, sweeping movement, he smoothed the large sheets of paper in front of him. The only sound was his slow, deep breathing while he focused on the scale drawings.

With his attention on the drawings, she was safe to study the beautiful man in front of her. She nodded her silent approval at the strong jaw line and high forehead. He seemed oblivious to the dark, unruly twist of hair that dangled enticingly over his brow. Fascinated, she watched as he traced the changes she had made from their last meeting. He paused, considering something for a moment and then looked up at her. The sudden shock of his dark eyes unnerved her, and blood rushed to her cheeks. Embarrassed, she pushed a loose wisp of hair from her brow.

"Why this beam . . . here?" he asked, pointing to the plan.

"Your father wants the staircase restored in the original marble stone." Short of breath, she paused briefly before she could continue. "So we will have to strengthen the support to carry the extra weight."

"Can you show me?"

Rachel took the plan from the table and walked toward the staircase with Alain following her. She paused at the steps and held the plans in front of her.

She looked up and indicated a point directly above them. "The joists will hang at that point from the beams you see on the plan here."

Alain stepped closer and stared intently over her shoulder at the plan. Her arms were outstretched at full length in front of her, holding the drawings in mid-air.

"From this point here?" he asked and leaned over her to indicate the area on the plan. Alain's chest touched her upper arm and her throat closed at the sudden warmth where their bodies touched. Rachel nodded twice in answer to his question and swallowed hard, but her mouth was dry. A light tremor ran through her hands and into the plans.

She spun into a slow spiral of desire. Alain's closeness burnt into her arm, and her heart skipped at the thought of his lips on her body. The unanswered craving left her dizzy and short of breath.

Keep it professional, now. Her feeble reminder came as an afterthought.

"Which beam?" he asked again, looking up to the ceiling.

She deftly folded the plan under her arm, anxious to get her wild emotions under control. She raised the folded plan and pointed to the wooden staircase. "Let me go and show you," she suggested to Alain.

Her breathing was shallow, and her heart hammered in her chest as she started up the fire-damaged staircase, taking care to avoid weakened treads and the loose handrail. Alain followed closely behind her.

She warned Alain over her shoulder, "Careful on the—"

With a loud, splintering crack, the weakened wood of the top step suddenly gave way under her foot, and she stumbled, trying to catch her balance. A firm hand shot out to steady her, and she staggered back against his body. Alain corrected his balance and gripped her body firmly against his.

She opened her eyes and exhaled. His chest pressed against her back, strong and warm. Memories flashed through her mind—his powerful body pressing down onto her, his gentle hands stroking her skin. Her heart fluttered wildly, and she turned around to face him, nervous and a little embarrassed in the tight circle of his embrace. "Thanks," she whispered, her voice low and shaky against his chest, but she could not bring herself to step out of his embrace.

Alain held her a little longer and then he lowered his head to her. Warm, firm lips found her mouth, and Rachel inhaled sharply at the sensation of his tongue dancing over her lips, probing, seeking. He pulled her closer to his body, and she closed her eyes as her breasts pressed against the firm muscles of his chest, the warmth of his body addictive. He placed a hand on her face, cupping her cheek, and then let it slide like silk down the nape of her neck. Her skin came alive, and sensations of electric pinpricks ran up her spine to nestle in her hair. Rachel shivered, and a soft sigh escaped from her throat. With a slight tilt of her head, she allowed him easier access to her mouth and started to meet the flickering probes of his tongue with hers.

His soft nip on her lower lip edged her to open wider, allowing him to feed his hungry urgency, and his tongue plunged into her mouth. She bunched a fistful of his long, dark hair and relaxed the tight muscles in her back, allowing her lower body to melt into his frame. Darting from lips to teeth, his tongue explored the soft depths of her mouth.

His hand traced the quivering ripples down the curve of her spine until it rested on her buttocks. He squeezed her so tightly against him that she could feel the hard heat of his arousal. A low groan escaped from deep in Alain's chest. He angled his hip to thrust her legs apart, and she met his thrust and pushed back.

She startled with shock at the loud crash of a door slamming shut. Muffled voices echoed from an empty room somewhere as the two contractors returned from the cigarette they had shared outside.

She pushed away from Alain abruptly, blinked twice, and, gathering herself, ran a hand through her ruffled hair. Looking up from straightening her clothes, she noticed a small, twisted smile playing on Alain's delicious lips. In an instant, she lost it. Angry at herself and her inability to stand up to his sexuality, she lashed out to hurt him.

"You hypocrite . . ."

Too late she realized her mistake. A dark, dangerous shadow flashed over his eyes, and his mouth snapped into a hard line. A small muscle flickered in anger under his left eye.

"Just add it to your itemized bill under entertainment," he snapped and stomped down the treacherous stairs in anger.

*

Furious with himself, Alain stormed out into the forecourt and sat down on a small wooden bench under an ancient chestnut tree.

Clearly, this wasn't going to work. Hypocrite, of all things. But she was right, he acknowledged. He had to get a grip on his emotions—his desires. Frustrated, he ran his hand over his jaw in an attempt to suppress the desire to step back into the chateau and kiss her into submission — to make passionate love to her.

"Get it into your head—she's married, Alain!" he shouted in frustrated anger. He was angry, his anger fueled by the dark history of his past

Agitated, he ran a hand roughly through his hair and exhaled slowly in an effort to calm down. He had to find a way to control this maddening urge inside him, a desire that grew stronger by the day. This crazy need to touch her, to caress her skin, to kiss her.

He sighed and leaned his elbows on his knees, staring morosely down at the ground between his feet. The problem, though, was not that simple, he finally admitted. It wasn't just her sensual body that appealed so strongly to him.

He constantly yearned for her company. She was intelligent and witty, strong-minded and independent—and gentle when she wanted to be. He smiled wryly. Everything he could ever wish for in a woman. He was falling in love—with the wrong woman. A married woman.

"And that cannot happen," he said with determination.

No, Rachel's life was with her husband and her kids, irrespective of his feelings for her. Regardless of the fact that she kissed him back, he thought bitterly. She had her family and he will not be responsible for destroying it. It needed to stop. He needed to kill these growing feelings inside him before it got out of hand.

"Kill the romance. Now," he whispered and swallowed hard.

Suddenly eager to get away from the chateau, Alain hurried over to his car. His decision was made. He would treat Rachel as the architect on the project. From now on, it would be strictly professional.

Chapter Sixteen

Rachel closed her eyes, breathed deeply and tried to slow her heartbeat.

"So much for keeping it professional," she said aloud. It was clear that working with Alain on this project was going to be much more difficult than she'd anticipated.

But why did he kiss me?

And why did I kiss him back?

She willed her mind to step methodically through her actions over the last couple of weeks, analyzing her behavior, critical of every word she said, every movement she made, every hint she might have left. Had she led him on? And if she had, what could she do to avoid a repeat of what just happened on the staircase?

Acutely aware of the terms under which Alain agreed to continue work with Swift & Simon, she didn't want to agitate the man any further. After all, he was her client.

Or was he?

Her contract was with Chateau Léon, signed by Eugene. Surely Alain couldn't simply cancel the contract if he was uncomfortable working with her. Or could he?

A low, dull headache began to take up residence in the back of her head, and Rachel leaned forward, closed her eyes, and pinched her nose.

"I fell, for crying out loud," she said with conviction. No need to be apologetic, or change her behavior. "You will just have to keep your hands in your pockets, Mr. Alain Léon," she muttered, irritation shallow in her voice.

"Ah, Rachel, you bring pleasure to my eyes and warmth to my soul." Her eyes shot wide open as Eugene's warm voice interrupted her thoughts. She turned and smiled bravely at him.

His hands trembled when he took her shoulders to kiss her on both cheeks. Rachel frowned—he was exhausted. She had tried to slow the pace and shorten the hours when Eugene worked with her, but he wouldn't have any of it. Now that the design was selected, it seemed almost as if he was rushing the project, urging Rachel on.

Eugene turned his attention to the drawing on the table. His stooped figure seemed so fragile, his shoulders so thin. He needed to rest. The work was sapping all his energy.

"Let's get some fresh air," she suggested gently, and took Eugene's bony hand in hers, willing him to accept her invitation. Eugene looked at her, a tired smile on his face, his deep blue eyes watery and a little sad.

She led them to a warm spot in the sun, and they sat down on a cast iron bench in the forecourt. In silence, Eugene crossed his legs and arms and let his gaze fall on the valley in front of them.

The faint, familiar smell of wood fire hung in the air. Farmers were busy pruning their vines, burning the dry, twisted clippings, sending long, lazy blue smoke columns into the sky. In the far distance, the majestic eagle-shaped rock on the island, just off La Ciotat, rose from the blue Mediterranean Sea, proudly poised as if surveying the horizon for prey. Ready to take flight.

Closer to them, the twin hilltop villages of La Cadiere and Le Castellet eagerly soaked up the mild, early spring sun, balanced precariously on the steep rock faces. Scattered, like patchwork against the hills and in the valleys, were the orderly rows of the region's vineyards.

Her gaze shifted to Eugene and noticed that he had closed his eyes. She remained absolutely still next to him. They sat for a while and then Eugene said, "I love this part of France."

"Tell me about the fire," Rachel asked gently, hoping to keep him resting in the sun a while longer.

Eugene sat, not moving. For a long moment, Rachel thought he was going to ignore her question. Then he cleared his throat.

"It was a dry summer, that year in 1984," Eugene began. "We were better off than the rest, having a spring in a deep ravine that still produced water till late in July."

He laughed quietly at some thought, and then continued. "The spring was our little secret meeting place. We would meet there as young lovers, swim in the cool water, and then do what young lovers do best. That was, until her mother put a stop to our little secret meetings."

He opened his eyes and Rachel noticed the glint of wetness.

"On our first night after Celine and I got married, we took a blanket and some champagne, and spent the night in each other's arms at that spring, staring up between the rock cliffs at the stars high above, until we fell asleep."

"You must have loved her a lot," Rachel said softly, almost afraid to interrupt him.

"Still do," he replied.

Rachel sucked in her breath involuntary. During the months she had worked with Eugene, he gave no indication that his wife was still alive. However, she sensed with growing certainty that something was amiss.

"No one knows how the fire started that night—something the insurance company liked to point out repeatedly in their counter arguments. The vines were dry and burned like paper, spreading quickly in the strong wind." Eugene shifted uneasily at the ghastly memory. "By the time we woke, the fire raged out of control, threatening the chateau. We tried to save the building, but eventually the west wing caught fire." Eugene coughed softly and looked out over the valley. "Our vineyards were destroyed, and I had to rebuild the estate from scratch. It was hard on us—very hard on us."

Eugene turned and looked at Rachel. She dropped her gaze, suddenly uncomfortable with the idea that Eugene was sharing his innermost secrets with her. Uncomfortable, because it gave her a view into the private life of the Léon family—the private life of Alain. She wanted to know no more. Resting her hand on Eugene's arm, she looked into his sad, wrinkled face and slowly shook her head from side to side.

"She left us that December." Eugene's voice continued with fresh determination, and Rachel sensed that the painful words Eugene was about to speak had been eating at him for years.

"I don't think she believed in me anymore—that I could rebuild the estate. That I could get us out of the financial nightmare that haunted our every night's sleep. So . . . she simply gave up on us." Eugene studied his left hand, turning the gold wedding band on his ring finger, deep in thought. "I came home late that afternoon to find she had already left for Canada. All she took with her was some clothes packed in one suitcase. Alain's nanny had Celine's last note for me."

"I'm so sorry, Eugene." She squeezed his arm lightly.

Eugene continued. "It was tough on Alain. He was only five, and I hoped he would never blame her. How could he? She was his mother?"

She looked at Eugene and recognized his pain—the pain caused by Celine's rejection. The same pain she'd experienced at Stuart's hands.

"So is Celine still in Canada?"

"Yes. When Alain turned fifteen he told me he wanted to visit his mother in Canada. I took him, but I could never bring myself to see Celine during that visit. I could not trust my own feelings."

"And you've never seen her since she left?"

"I've tried. More than once, believe me. Inside me, it is like two raging dragons, clawing at each other in battle. The white dragon fights to protect my love for Celine. The black dragon fights for my hate to win. So far, the white dragon has survived. I don't know what will happen if I lay eyes on Celine again."

With a shaky voice Eugene continued, "Alain didn't blame his mother, but he did grow up hating the man who cost him his mother."

She sat upright, alarmed. "Another man . . ."

"Yes, her lover, Thomas."

"So Celine had a lover. And that's why she abandoned you and Alain?"

"Yes, and Thomas was also married. Two months after they left for Canada, Thomas' young wife jumped to her death from a high cliff just outside La Ciotat."

"What a terrible tragedy."

"Yes, it was a terrible thing for a young boy to experience—I was too busy rebuilding the estate." He searched Rachel's eyes, seeking her understanding. "It pained me when I saw all that despair in my son. Growing up with anger in his heart is not something I wanted for him. It took a long time, but eventually Alain let go of his hate. But it left a scar. Adultery destroys lives."

A cold hand gripped Rachel's heart.

Adultery. She needed time to think.

"Oh, Eugene, all this must have been so painful."

"That is why I'm tackling this project, Rachel. For years, I couldn't bring myself to rebuild the house where we were so happy. Now, I know I must do it. I must complete the circle."

"I'm glad to know you will live here again, and that I have helped to make that possible."

"Oh, no, Rachel, I'm not doing this for me—I'm doing it for my Alain."

Squinting against the sun, he looked at Rachel. "This chateau has been empty and sad for much too long now—it's time for its halls to be filled once more with the sounds of happiness, the laughter of children."

Too late, she tried to hide the dark shadow of regret moving across her eyes. She held her breath, but knew Eugene's sharp eyes spotted it when he sat up and asked, "What? You think I'm a fool—an old man with a crazy dream? You don't agree with me?"

She studied his deeply lined face, the warm, friendly eyes, now questioning her intently, and chose her words with care.

"Oh, I agree with you, Eugene—completely." She lifted her face to take in the majestic sandstone building in front of her. A sad smile played on her lips. "This beautiful chateau should be the home to happiness, a family, the laughter of children . . . "

Eugene slapped a heavy hand on his one knee and said firmly, "Oh, it will, Rachel, it will." Then, with a quick wink, "All we need to do is find him the right wife—he's so damn picky. That is the real conundrum." Eugene stood and massaged his back. "I'm ready to go home," he said and walked to his car.

Rachel remained seated on the bench. The information Eugene had shared with her looped through her mind.

Adultery—it flashed through her mind. His vehement reaction and "no *buts*, *ifs*, or *ands*" made more sense now. It was rooted in the scars left by his mother's adultery.

She smiled wryly and the irony was not lost on her. Stuart, her spineless husband, had left her—deserted her and their two babies. When she met Alain in Monaco that evening, they had been separated for more than three years. Her marriage was long dead—she was married to a ghost, and adultery was an impossibility.

But Alain never paused to hear her side of the story.

"No *buts*, *ifs*, or *ands*," she repeated Alain's words to herself. And then continued, "But now I'm no longer married, Mr. Léon."

Chapter Seventeen

Rachel arrived at the chateau early the next morning. The low, menacing shape of a vintage Aston Martin was parked in the shade under a tree. She sighed heavily with solemn recognition.

Alain's.

Killing the engine, she remained seated in her vehicle, her mind heavy. Hot, humid air seemed to rush in and replace the cold air from the silenced air conditioner in seconds. It was not quite nine o'clock.

Her gaze drifted to the chateau's open front door. I don't have the energy for another encounter, she thought and closed her eyes. They were scratchy from little sleep. And here she was, confused and undecided, despite spending most of the evening tossing and turning in her bed. She unclipped the safety belt, but remained seated.

I'm divorced now—no longer married. So, should I tell him? Then doubt settled again. *Will it even make a difference? In theory I was still married that night in Monaco. Does he even care? This is such a mess.*

Suddenly annoyed, she spoke out loud, "Adultery. And I've been celibate for three years!"

Then, with a determined twist of her mouth, she snapped the vanity mirror down and checked her makeup. "I will tell him—I will tell him I'm not married anymore," she muttered with false bravado. Gathering her energy, Rachel extracted herself from the vehicle, grabbed her handbag, and headed up the stairs toward the front door.

"Hello!" she greeted the empty house, and nervously ran a hand to straighten the lavender, cross-over dress she was wearing. Her voice was a trifle too cheerful.

"I'm in here!" His voice boomed from the west wing. A hollow feeling came to her stomach, but with a determined grip on her handbag, Rachel made her way to the library.

"Good morning," he greeted her stiffly when she entered the large room. Alain was dressed in casual trousers, soft leather loafers, and a black linen shirt. He seemed distant, almost aloof. Cold even.

Bright light entered the library through a series of floor-to-ceiling paneled windows. Heavy bookshelves and rich cherry wood paneled walls created an atmosphere of warmth and luxury.

She turned her head to take in the vast collection of different materials displayed in front of her. Most of the room was filled with an organized assortment of sample materials, primarily from France, but she also noted some exquisite samples from Italy and Spain. In the far corner, a large pile of printed color brochures documented the latest features of a choice selection of expensive heavy appliances, sophisticated electronics, and alarm systems.

Rachel's heeled sandals clicked on the worn oak parquet flooring as she slowly made her way through the room, her sweeping gaze taking in the materials.

She laid her hand lightly on the rich, creamy, veined marble sample on the table. "I see you've been busy."

"And you've already made your selection." His gaze briefly dropped to her hand on the marble sample.

So this is how we are going to play it. Civil, polite and strictly professional—how utterly boring. She frowned lightly and she scolded herself.

"Yes, this is probably my favorite color for the bathroom flooring, but in the end you will be the one living here. You will have to make the final decisions." The tone of her voice was even and businesslike. With a sweeping motion of her hand, she included the vast selection of sample materials stacked across the room.

A slight smile played on his handsome face. With effort, she tore her eyes away from the debonair little scar on his upper lip. Surprised by the impulse to run her tongue over it, she clenched the sharp nails of her left hand deep into her palm in a warning to herself.

Behave, Rachel, she mused despondently.

Alain's brow wrinkled in thought while he briefly pondered her words, his jaw cupped in his hand as his elbow rested on the table. He sat in silence for a moment, and then seemed to make a quick decision.

"I have an idea," he suggested, raising his dark eyes to her. "Why don't you pick all your favorites—floor tiles, bathroom tiles, hardware, paint color, trims, balustrades—the whole lot. Once you've done that, I can simply approve or reject your selections—add my own touch where I feel it is needed."

Preoccupied, Rachel twirled a loose lock of hair in her fingers while she considered Alain's unexpected suggestion. He was giving her complete freedom to finish the chateau to her taste, trusting her judgment in the selection of tiles, flooring, color, drapes, appliances—everything. Unusual, since he was going to be the one living with her selections. But what a thrill that would be.

"Sure, I can do that." She made her decision, intrigued with the prospect of finishing the chateau to reflect her own style and taste.

"Great." And with that, Alain grabbed one of the rickety bentwood chairs, propped it against the far wall, and planted himself on it. He crossed his long legs at the ankles and leaned back comfortably in the chair, busying himself with his iPhone.

"Now—you want me to make the selections now?"

"Sure, why not?" he replied with raised brows as if surprised by her hesitation.

Rachel stared at Alain for a moment. He was serious about this, she decided. Shaking her head, she removed the scarf from her hair to put it aside along with her purse.

Well, why not?

She completed a slow circle, taking in the vast array of materials and brochures in front of her, her eyes focused in concentration. Working her way meticulously through the materials, she started selecting her top three choices in each category, starting with the flooring. Flooring first—the base of everything that follows.

Soon Rachel had lost herself in a fantasy world of make-believe, flirting with choices in color, textures and materials. The options were vast, as Alain had arranged samples ranging from stone, wood, and steel, natural and engineered, hand-made, custom, and mass-produced, local and imported.

Her fingers darted from sample to sample, her mind creating first one theme, then ditching it all, only to start again. She was sensitive to maintain the authenticity of the period in which the chateau was built, but determined to find warmth and comfort as well. She wanted the finished chateau to offer its owner a place to live in comfort—a home.

A home—Alain's home.

This would be the home where Alain and his wife would live one day, she realized with alarm. She risked a quick glance in Alain's direction. He sat, his body relaxed in the chair, dark hair tumbling over his face, concentrating on reading his messages. Pain stabbed at her heart, and for a moment, she toiled with the thought of telling him that she was not married anymore. Tell him that she was separated from Stuart when they met that evening in Monaco. The words formed in her mind: *Alain, just in case you wanted to know, I'm not married anymore.* But that sounded desperate and feeble, and Alain's aloofness discouraged her. What if is she was wrong? What if he didn't feel the same way about her and she was rejected—again. Courage drained from her, and she shut her mind to the thought, concentrating on the task of selecting materials.

Alain watched her surreptitiously from where he sat against the wall, using his phone to catch up on his email and the latest financials. An excited glow radiated from her while she worked feverishly to select the appropriate materials for the flooring, bathrooms, kitchen, and walls.

Every so often, she would stop, her face drawn in concentration, contemplating the options spread out on the table in front of her. At these moments, he would hold his breath in anticipation, waiting for the instant when she would pinch her lower lip between her thumb and index finger, squeezing the firm, sensuous flesh, rolling it deliciously so that he almost groaned aloud in agony and lust. Then she would turn with a firm shake of her head, mumbling to herself to search her neatly stacked piles of samples for one to replace the one she'd just discarded.

A light sweat formed on his brow, but it couldn't be entirely attributed to the oppressive humidity of the day. He wiped his brow, inhaled deeply and closed his mind to the swirls of passion waking in his loins. He'd made his decision, and would stick to it.

"You hungry?" he asked, his voice clear and sudden in the big room.

Rachel looked up, somewhat confused at Alain's question. Then, glancing at her watch, opened her mouth in surprise at how fast the morning had slipped by. A hollow feeling from her stomach reminded her of the scant yogurt and coffee she enjoyed for breakfast, a long time ago.

She nodded.

"Care to join me for lunch in Cassis then?"

She pushed the samples she was arranging to one side and considered Alain's invitation. A quick lunch. She was hungry; he was hungry. In London, she wouldn't think twice about dining with a client. "Why not," she replied. "Give me a minute to freshen up."

Chapter Eighteen

Alain maneuvered the low car down the rutted gravel lane toward the main road and headed south. The day's unusual heat was sweltering, but the open top allowed the sea breeze to provide them with some welcome relief. Soon they were following the twisty road down toward the harbor town. Alain parked in front of a quaint restaurant in a quiet side road.

Rachel glanced up at the restaurant entrance, hidden under a lush growth of ancient jasmine that engulfed the small front yard. Alain ushered her toward the entrance with a light hand on her lower back. She flipped her hair back and tried to ignore the pleasant sensation of his touch.

They stepped from the searing humidity into the cool, welcoming interior of the restaurant. Rachel removed her sunglasses and took in the tasteful décor, elegantly laid tables, and soft, artistic lighting. Saliva pooled in her mouth at the delicious smells of grilled fish, roasted garlic, and freshly baked bread.

"Monsieur Léon, *bienvenue.*" The short, portly owner made his way over to them, his face beaming with pride. When Alain introduced Rachel, she noticed a familiarity between the two men that spoke of respect and friendship.

"*Suivez-moi, si'l vous plait,*" the owner requested and they followed him to a secluded table against the far wall.

"You come here often?" Rachel smiled at Alain after they were seated.

"I do—I bought the restaurant two years ago when the previous owner retired." He nodded his head to the entrance. "Michelle was our catering manager at the chateau—weddings and functions. But he always had bigger dreams—"

"So, you helped him out." She completed the tale. Alain nodded, smiled at her, and dropped his gaze to study the menu in his hands. She shook her head, and concentrated on her menu.

Alain ordered sparkling water and a pale rosé wine from the famous Var region.

"Ready to order?" he asked as their waitress approached.

"Yes." Looking up at the young waitress, Rachel ordered a fresh garden salad and the catch of the day.

"You'll enjoy that," Alain replied and ordered his meal.

"*Santé.*" He raised his glass to her. Rachel returned the gesture in kind, a warm smile on her lips. She took a sip of the ice-cold wine, savoring the tangy taste of peach on her palate, and sat back in her chair with an appreciative sigh.

Alain studied her with dark, shielded eyes. He sat, leaning lightly on his elbows, his wide shoulders framing his chest. Strong hands, sensually crisscrossed with healthy veins, twirled the glass of wine on the cotton tablecloth in front of him. The glass appeared fragile in the sun-browned, powerful hand.

"Eugene seems anxious to push ahead with the project," she ventured, selecting neutral territory. Alain nodded once, but she couldn't tell whether he nodded in agreement to her statement, or in appreciation of her safe topic of discussion. He exhaled, seemingly made a decision, and sat back, relaxed.

"He's always been like that. Get him started on something, and he won't rest until it is done."

"Like when he rebuilt the estate after the fire?"

A quick shadow passed over Alain's dark eyes, but he recovered with a warm smile. "Yes, I was only five, but I remember how he slaved to save us from bankruptcy. I don't know any other man that could do that. " His last words were softer, warmer.

"You've done well to expand the wealth of the Léon family," Rachel suggested.

Alain's dark eyes pierced her without any acknowledgement.

Then he smiled, the warmth returning to his eyes. "True, but we might be bankrupt again after we've paid your bill," he joked lightly, and the tense knot in her shoulders released as she relaxed. He had moved on from yesterday, choosing not to make anything of it. That was good, was it not? Now they could get on with the project, keeping it all professional—strictly business only.

Should I tell him? Indecision was driving her crazy.

Their salads arrived and Alain refilled their glasses. Over the chilled wine and the crisp, fresh salad, their conversation drifted to more interesting topics.

Alain's charismatic persona kicked in and soon he had Rachel sharing stories of her times as a student, her career as a young, starry-eyed architect, and her trusted friend and business partner, Peter, back in London. Conversation came easy and unforced, but Rachel sensed that Alain was deliberately avoiding the sensitive topics of their relationship, or that disastrous evening in Monaco. Or their kiss of yesterday.

A light blush covered Rachel's cheeks at the memory of their kiss, and for a moment she considered telling Alain about her divorce again. She frowned lightly, irritated at herself for struggling to find the right words. More challenging, however, was finding the right time during their conversation. Alain seemed determined on keeping the conversation platonic. She would sound so desperate, blurting out her marital status.

Maybe it didn't matter to him anymore.

A flutter of disappointment shadowed her mind and Rachel rallied to flash a brave smile at Alain. Time she moved on, like Alain had.

Their main course arrived in a gastronomic aroma of steam. Rachel sampled the royal dorade and rolled her eyes to a close in silent appreciation of the delicious taste of grilled fresh fish, lemon, garlic, and caramelized fennel. The chef had deboned the delicate fish, and it was served with a small helping of wild rice and cooked vegetables.

Heaven, she thought, and noticed Alain's gaze transfixed on her mouth. He cleared his throat and raised his glass. "To friendship—and the project," he proposed.

"I'll drink to that." Rachel raised her glass in accord, but the nagging twitch between her shoulders had returned. Despite the attraction, Alain's message was clear.

He dropped his gaze and focused on his meal. The flatware appeared delicate in his strong hands as he deftly worked his fork in the deep bowl of al dente seafood pasta. The strong rake of his wide shoulders filled the folds of his shirt, his masculine frame appearing almost ominous dressed in black. Below loosely rolled shirtsleeves, the bronze of his forearms danced and rippled in the soft light as he scooped cooked mussels from the shells.

Rachel's eyes were fixed on the strong, long fingers, twirling the pasta on his fork and scooping the rich pasta sauce in one movement. For a brief moment, a sliver of pasta dangled deliciously between his sensual lips, and in that instant Rachel wanted to lean forward and suck if from his mouth, tempting him to bewitch her once again with the magic of his tongue. With a wild shiver, she realized that a relationship based on business only with this man would drive her insane.

"Your food good?" he asked, his eyes remaining on his plate, and Rachel shifted, embarrassed. She pushed her thoughts aside.

"D-delicious, thank you," she mustered, clearing her throat.

Sometime later, after their meal, Rachel declined dessert and Alain ordered coffee. The kick of caffeine seemed to have a calming effect on the wild passions raging inside her, and Rachel relaxed, feeling more at ease.

At Alain's suggestion, they went for a slow stroll through the small fishing harbor. A blustery wind had sprung up, chasing dark, threatening clouds up the steep cliffs overlooking the sleepy village. The harbor was filled with row upon row of brightly painted fishing boats, hiding from the threatening wind in the safety of the port. Rachel's eyes drifted over the different shapes, sizes, and colors of the boats, each one kept in pristine condition by its doting captain.

"My father used to bring me here as a kid, early in the mornings." Alain's gaze drifted to the dock. "We would buy our fish fresh from the boats."

They turned and walked back to Alain's vehicle. That Alain had not once mentioned his mother in all the time she'd known him was not lost on Rachel.

Alain drove them back up the steep, twisting road out of Cassis. Rachel sat back in her seat, lifted her head so the wind took her hair and closed her eyes. The gusty wind tugged wildly at her loose dress and whipped her hair into a crazy flag of flying chestnut and gold. At the T-junction, Alain, momentarily distracted by the sensuous curve of Rachel's breast revealed by the blustering wind, stalled the engine. Clear, boisterous laughter rang from Rachel while embarrassment flashed briefly on Alain's cheeks.

"Can happen to the best of us," he tried to reason weakly, but Rachel's deliberate light snicker continued as she teased him.

"Fine, lady—you drive." He jumped from the seat and bowed at the open door, inviting her to take up his position.

"No, no, I was just teasing," Rachel backtracked, shaking her head in laughter.

"Well, for that you must pay," Alain insisted mockingly, inclining his head to the vacated driver's seat.

"You're sure?" Rachel asked, both nervous and excited. At Alain's insistent nod, she scuttled around the vehicle to take up a position behind the wheel. She turned the key and the powerful engine fired to settle into a deep burble.

"Make a right turn here," Alain instructed. "There is something I want to show you . . . "

With a confident but explorative push on the gas pedal, Rachel pulled away, following Alain's directions up the steep, curving

Route des Cretes toward the east of Cassis. With each twist and turn, Rachel's sense of the vehicle's power, grip, and balance grew, and so did her confidence. Soon the engine growled and they roared up the steep mountain, Rachel's high-pitched whoop echoing from the cliffs as she propelled them to the apex with controlled ease.

"Impressive. Another hidden talent," Alain nodded his appreciation at her when she parked the vehicle at the summit.

A deep, rolling thunder interrupted them, and Alain jumped from the car, running to the lookout point. His feet planted wide and firm, he stood tall and strong on the crest as the wild winds buffeted his clothes. His black hair a pirate's flag flying in the wind.

"Come!" he called to her against the ear-splitting crash of thunder as the electric storm unleashed its power over Cassis far below him.

Rachel scrambled toward Alain, a protective arm raised against the strong, blustery wind. She came to a halt next to him and inhaled sharply at the spectacular view. Almost a thousand feet below them, the sea had been whipped into a frenzy of angry waves, capped with wild white caps. Narrow shafts of golden-gray sunlight shone down valiantly onto Cassis in a brave battle against the dark, rolling clouds crashing into the mountains above the fishing village.

Rachel jolted in fright when a thunderous crash announced the arrival of the electric storm. Lightning sparked blue-white and crackled dangerously as it released its awesome power, raking the granite face of the patient mountain.

She watched with bated breath as fear and awe washed over her. She shivered, but it was not from cold, for the oppressive humidity still clung to her body.

"Hold on, it's a long drop down," Alain cautioned, and extended his hand. Strong, supple fingers entwined with hers. Her hand was small in the power of his grip. She froze, amazed at the warm comfort washing over her. Hand in hand, wordless, legs planted firmly against the strong wind, they watched the spectacle at their feet, the raw power of nature released in all its might.

Thunder exploded and lightning executed its deadly dance against the cliffs. Strangely, despite the imminent danger, she felt safe with her hand in Alain's tight grip. It was a feeling she had missed so dearly. And now she would miss it even more. She winched sharply at the splat of a warm, fat raindrop against her face.

"Come," Alain shouted against the wind, and they ran back to raise the hood on the convertible just as the first drops plopped in the dust at their feet.

*

Amazingly, the air was dry and warm when Alain parked the car at the chateau a while later. They sat in silence for a moment, unwilling to part at the realization that, going forward, things would be different between them.

"Thanks for lunch, Alain," she whispered, "and for a great day."

Alain turned to face her in the confines of the vehicle, a smile lingering on his lips. He lifted his gaze to indicate the chateau. "Thanks for what you're doing here, Rachel."

The compliment took her by surprise, and with some apprehension, she searched his eyes for confirmation. His steady gaze met hers and she found the truth—he was truly pleased with the project.

A happy client—mission accomplished, she thought with a cynical smile. She looked up at the tall walls of the chateau, trying to ignore the dull sadness growing in her chest, and made a quick decision. She had to tell him now.

Turning to face Alain, she started, "About my marriage . . ."

Alain recoiled and interrupted abruptly. "Rachel, stop. I invited you for lunch to apologize for yesterday—and Monaco. It should never have happened. Let's work to finish the project. *D'accord*?"

She cringed at Alain's harsh words. She dropped her gaze, and hiding her feelings, replied bravely, "Sounds fair."

Humiliation rushed her. A sudden need to be alone gripped her, and she nodded goodbye, opened her door, and hurried toward her own vehicle. She just had to get away. Away from the burning feeling in her chest while warm tears threatened. Away from the pain—pain caused by the realization that Alain was lost to her. Salty tears welled in her eyes, and she swallowed hard to prevent them from spilling onto her cheeks. No tears to show her sadness. He would not see her cry, and she swallowed hard at the painful lump in her throat.

She unlocked her car, thankful for the relative solitude, and shut the door with a heavy clunk. Fumbling with the starter as warm tears flowed unchecked from her eyes, Rachel accepted the cruel reality.

It's over. How ironic, now that she was finally divorced.

"Why . . . why did I have to fall in love with this man?" she sobbed, before she finally managed to get the engine started.

Chapter Nineteen

Rachel sat motionless, fingers tapping the wheel, the slow tick of the cooling engine and the lonely coo of the mourning doves the only sounds in the otherwise quiet forecourt.

Black and ominous, leaning on its side-stand next to Eugene's vehicle, she made out the low, feline-like shape of a powerful motorcycle. For a second her heart raced, wild with excitement. Then, recalling Alain's aversion for motorcycles, she slumped back in her seat, disappointed.

No, it wouldn't be Alain's — in the last six weeks, she'd not rested her eyes on his beautiful face once. Ever since their lunch in Cassis, he had made every effort to avoid physical contact with Rachel, and she had not seen Alain or spoken to him. It was as if he'd moved to a different continent. All communication regarding the project was conducted via email.

"Well, he *was* on a different continent," she mumbled. Alain had flown to San Francisco on business last week, and she had no idea when he would be back.

Move on, Rachel, like he's done, she tried to encourage herself, but deep inside Rachel knew it wouldn't be that simple.

She reached for the drawings from the back seat, locked the car, and with a last, quizzical glance at the motorcycle, climbed the worn marble stairs to the front door.

At the creak of the heavy door opening, Eugene straightened from where he was leaning over the drawings laid out on the temporary desk.

"Ah ha, my favorite moment of the day." He pushed a bony hand through his thin, rumpled hair.

Rachel crossed the foyer, the hollow echoes of her shoes on the wooden floorboards bouncing from the high ceilings in the empty room.

"Glad you're here, Rachel." Eugene nodded toward the stone tile sample on the table next to the drawing. "I've been studying the selection you've put together, but Marque's been very distracting. Let me introduce you—"

Marque looked up from the plans he was studying, a surprised look on his face. Then he smiled warmly at Rachel. "Oh, but we've met before. Hi, Rachel."

"Yes," Rachel confirmed. "Nice to see you again, Marque." At the puzzled look on Eugene's face, Marque explained, "Last May in Monaco — Alain's yacht."

Eugene nodded and continued with his struggle to roll the plans together. He puffed his cheeks frustrated at his fruitless efforts and Marque gently took the plans from his hands. After rolling them neatly, he slid the drawings into the plastic storage tube and handed them to Eugene. "There you go." Marque winked at Rachel and continued in jest, "As a friend of Alain's, I unfortunately have to deal with this grumpy old man ever so often."

"I don't see enough of you—you're too much in love with that boat of yours," Eugene fired back.

"It's a yacht, not a boat."

Eugene chuckled and shouldered the tube. "Rachel, I have a meeting at the mayor's office in an hour. Why don't you meet me for lunch at Chez Du Pont's?"

"Thanks. See you there, Eugene."

As Eugene left, Rachel turned back to Marque. "So you're not just a sailor, but also interested in architecture?"

Marque smiled, shook his head and crossed his arms lightly over his chest. She noticed the telltale signs of the ocean-loving sailor in the fine wrinkles around his eyes, the hard calluses on his hands, the strong back and sinewy arms from winching lines in strong winds. They shared the same love for the ocean, and she missed that sensation—the sensation of being one with the elements out in the open sea.

"So, what is she, this *Pure Joy* of yours?" Rachel asked invitingly, eager to learn more about Marque and his true love.

"She's a Swan 45. Do you know anything about sailing?" Marque responded keenly, quick to sense a kindred spirit.

"A little," Rachel admitted, and dropped her head to guard her smile.

"Would you like to sail with us?" Marque asked.

"Sure," Rachel responded, knowing this was going somewhere.

Marque smiled, and, leaning forward, rested his elbows lightly on the dusty table. He tented his huge hands in front of his face, and then, making his decision, lifted his eyes to look at Rachel.

"I bought her three years ago and re-fitted her completely. Alain and I sailed her in the Rolex Swan Cup in Italy last year—came in fourth in our class," he announced, watching Rachel's face for her reaction.

Rachel knew Marque wasn't boasting—he was merely establishing the level of sailing he competed in. He was also determining her competency and skill level.

"When's your next race?" Rachel asked, meeting his challenge with confidence.

"Saturday—we're competing in the St. Tropez Cup." He smiled, little devils of joy dancing in his steel grey eyes. "And I'm short a deck hand."

"Then I'm your man—or rather girl," she announced, excited about the prospect of sailing competitively again.

With a loud thud of his hand on the table, he exclaimed, "Magnificent—you are my best-looking deckhand ever. Do you need any gear?"

Rachel pinched her lower lip, briefly considering her options. Appropriate clothing would be essential, but all her sailing gear was stowed on her father's yacht in Plymouth. If she acted fast, he could have it shipped overnight.

"No, I'll bring my own gear, thanks," she made up her mind.

"Done. Make sure you go to bed early on Friday—I want everyone on board by eight. You can get a ride with Alain—"

"N-no, I can drive myself," Rachel injected hastily, anxious to avoid spending an hour alone with Alain on the drive down to St. Tropez. She couldn't trust herself to hide her emotions. And she certainly didn't want Alain to think she was seeking out his company.

Marque snorted, amused, and waved a dismissive hand in the air. "Rachel, you won't find parking anywhere near St. Tropez on Saturday, and I don't want to risk having to set sail without you." His steel gray eyes held her gaze. "Alain has reserved parking at the marina, and you're practically on his way—just outside Cassis, right? It's settled—see you bright and early," he said decisively, and with that, Marque ended the discussion, grabbed his helmet, and headed for the door, whistling a happy tune as he fished his mobile from his top pocket.

*

"Good, you're back from Frisco," Marque's brusque greeting came when Alain answered his phone. "I've got good news—found a replacement for our injured Suzy. Rachel is going to stand in," he finished before Alain could interject. "Told her you'll pick her up around six," he continued, taking advantage of Alain's stunned silence to unload the whole lot in one go.

"What are you trying to do, Marque?" Alain seethed, his voice menacing.

"You should thank me, big guy—you've been dreaming about this girl for long enough now," Marque countered.

With deliberate control, Alain inhaled, and then continued in a measured voice, "You don't understand, Marque. She's married, and I've made a decision—our relationship's been purely professional now and—"

"Yes," Marque interjected. "Professional for the last six weeks it was, and you've been a miserable sob ever since. So what if she's married? You can't seriously believe this guy—this husband—still means anything to her?"

Encouraged by Alain's silence, Marque pushed on, "Have you seen him at all? Has your father met him—has anyone seen him in all the time she's been here in Provence? Tell you what—why don't you ask her about this so-called husband of hers? Find out how much he really means to her if that bothers you so much." At Alain's silence, Marque continued, "That's got you thinking, hasn't it?"

"Fine, I'll pick her up at six," he agreed reluctantly, imagining the smirk on his friend's face. Marque had manipulated the situation so that it would be rude of him to refuse. Without a further word, Alain rang off.

He puffed his cheeks, exhaled, and ran a hand roughly through his dark hair. His eyes were scratchy, and the tablet he swallowed minutes ago had done nothing to relieve his thumping headache. The long flight back from San Francisco was murder. Irritation niggled at him as he reflected on Marque's comments. To his credit, Marque might have a point. Rachel had not mentioned her husband once. Further, reflecting on their evening in Monaco, adultery didn't seem to fit her personality.

A soft cough interrupted his thoughts and Eugene stepped into his office. With a heavy sigh, his father sat down in the luxury of the deep leather chair across from his desk.

"Good trip?"

Alain was aware of his father's deep blue eyes searching his face. "Yes, thanks. All went as planned," Alain replied, running a hand slowly over his brow and down his face. He waited, sensing his father's motive for this conversation wasn't to discuss the results of his latest business trip.

"Everything under control then?"

Alain noticed the invitation in Eugene's remark. "What's on your mind, Father?" He pushed back to recline his lengthy frame in the chair, crossing his legs at the ankles. This could take a while.

"Rachel—you've met her before," Eugene inquired.

Alain sighed heavily and dropped his gaze, studying his hands intently as he gathered his thoughts. Then he raised his eyes to Eugene and simply said, "Monaco." The word brought back uncomfortable memories. "She's married," Alain replied in answer to Eugene's silent question.

Understanding flashed in Eugene's eyes.

"Hmm . . . " Eugene replied, but his eyes never wavered. "And she's happy in this marriage? She's loved and cherished by this husband of hers? She feels safe and secure with him? And he treasures her? You know all these things?"

Alain narrowed his eyes at his father's words. The mere thought of Rachel in someone else's arms pained him. But the thought of Rachel not being treated as the special person she was—or being mistreated—those thoughts gave rise to a deep anger in Alain.

He exhaled slowly and studied his father's face.

Eugene returned his gaze and added, "You know I'll never condone unfaithfulness. It pains me to say this, Alain, but Rachel is nothing like Celine. She would never leave her children. You should talk to her." And with that Eugene stood and walked from the room.

Chapter Twenty

The eastern sky was still tinted a light peach when Alain held the door for Rachel to seat herself. She wore no jewelry or rings, and had dressed sensibly for the day of sailing awaiting them. Rachel handed her leather grip to Alain and he stowed it in the trunk. It was heavy, with the right clothing for any sailing weather, thanks to her father's quick action in shipping her sailing gear by overnight courier.

Alain paused before he fired the powerful engine, both hands on the wheel, and turned to face her. She waited, watching him in silence. The past months of tireless work, side by side, had forged a strong bond between them—despite the recent reserved, professional atmosphere. Lately Alain had become more intense, almost guarded. At times, she caught him staring at her with apparent indecision and frustration flashing in his eyes.

After their lunch in Cassis, Rachel had decided to follow Alain's example, suppressing her feelings to keep their relationship purely professional. At night, in the safety of her house, she could let her guard down, allowing the wicked, sensual images to infiltrate her mind. Images of his broad chest under a soft, cotton shirt, images of his muscular shoulders, tapering to his narrow hips, images of his strong arms. It would feel so good to be held by this strong, confident man.

But that was not to be—this was over, she mused and fastened her seatbelt with a determined action. She waited, patiently. Alain, once again, seemed to consider something.

"Ready?" he finally asked, and she nodded.

"I'm impressed—Marque told me you've sailed competitively in

Cowes Week on your father's yacht," he opened neutrally and fired the engine.

"Yes, but we didn't place well in the end—our navigation system failed on the second day."

Alain nodded in silent understanding.

"Arianne taking care of Iain and Mia?"

Rachel shot a surprised look in Alain direction. How bizarre—he remembered their names. "Yes," she replied, a little flustered. Then she added, pouting, "But I probably won't be missed—she spoils them rotten."

*

The wind was warm at a steady twenty-two knots when Alain and Rachel arrived in St. Tropez. On the horizon, a line of bright white sails in tight formation told the story of a fierce battle out at sea, yachts strategically jockeying for position to optimize the wind.

The marina was crammed with yachts, long masts bobbing and swaying, seemingly impatient to start the race as the metallic clangs of their halyards edged them on. Rachel shielded her eyes and stared at *Pure Joy*'s tall, dominating mast where she was moored along the wooden jetty.

"Permission to come aboard," she announced half joking when they reached the sleek yacht, bobbing impatiently at its mooring lines. Marque straightened from where he was plotting a course at the chart table, a determined look in his eyes. He seemed eager to discuss strategy with Alain. Selecting the right sails for the wind conditions would be crucial and could make the difference between edging out an extra knot, or a colorful explosion as the sail was blown to tatters. Marque extended his hand to help her onboard.

"Welcome on *Pure Joy*, Rachel." Then, leaning into her, he

welcomed her with a warm hug after she stepped onto the teak deck.

With quick efficiency Marque introduced Rachel to the rest of the crew—Jean and his wife Sophie, Pierre and his fiancée Yolande, and Christophe and Pascale. "Stow your gear and let's get the show started."

*

Rachel appeared back on deck moments later and Alain inhaled sharply. She had pleated her hair in a tight French plait in preparation for the task ahead, and it emphasized her high cheekbones. His gaze drifted slowly to take in her fine neckline. Her skin had gained a soft, honey-colored glow since she arrived in Provence six months ago.

She was dressed in charcoal quick-dry shorts that showed the perfect shape of her tight buttocks and long legs, and a white, fast-wicking crew top.

His eyes wandered briefly to the inviting shape of her breasts, and, remembering the night in Monaco, the image of her bare, hardened buds flashed through his mind. His pulse rushed and he breathed deeply, suddenly in need of more air, and he busied himself with the unnecessary task of securing a halyard to the jib with an overhand knot.

Marque took Rachel by the elbow and steered her toward Alain. "Alain, can you allocate Rachel while I radio race control?"

Alain focused on gathering the jib sheet into a neat coil in an over-arm motion, acutely aware of Rachel's quizzical expression. He hooked the coiled sheet onto a cleat and finally looked up to face Rachel's eyes.

"So, where do you want me?"

His heart thumped as her question provoked an image of a naked Rachel pinned under him, the tender flesh of her exposed breasts silky smooth to his touch, hardened nipples inviting him.

Blood flushed red in Rachel's neck and ears as she suddenly realized the double meaning of her question.

Alain studied Rachel, hands on hips, balanced on the balls of her feet, as she absorbed the gentle sway of the deck under her feet. Anticipation thrilled through him at the thought of having her so close for the whole day. She looked radiant and gorgeous, the wind playing with a stray lock of hair on her cheek. He had the sudden urge to tuck it away gently, stroking her smooth skin. Alain pushed a hand through his hair, grimaced and wrestled his lust down onto the deck.

"Why don't you take up position as main trimmer?" he suggested on impulse, hoping that by placing her at the stern he would not be so distracted by her presence.

Rachel nodded in agreement, grabbed her waterproof jacket, and made her way to the stern. Alain busied himself with another jib sheet, sneaking a quick glance at the perfect shape of Rachel's firm buttocks as she stepped lightly across the rolling deck.

It was going to be a long day.

*

By the time the warning gun fired, Marque had briefed the crew on their positions and the outline of the course. Rachel watched the faces of the other crewmembers while they moved under power toward the race committee boat bobbing in the distance. Rising excitement tingled in her stomach when Marque walked them through the strategy he and Alain had selected. She glanced at the high-end equipment and custom-made composite sails, and was again reminded of the importance of this event—especially for Marque and Alain. To them, this yacht was more than just a vessel to enjoy—it was honed to perfection with the sole purpose of winning. Their competitive nature would not accept anything but first place today, and she shivered at the thrill of the race lying ahead, confident in her ability to help this team achieve that goal.

The competing yachts approached the anchored boat of the racing committee in tight formation, their skippers glancing nervously upward to read the wind on their sails. Alain and Marque watched the competition, as they plotted to position *Pure Joy*. The minutes ticked off toward the start and the skipper's orders on the yachts took on a new urgency. Their sharp commands rang out above the wind, deliberate in their quests to jockey for position, timing their runs with the common objective of placing their vessels on the perfect tack when the gun sounded. In the chaos before the gun, the yachts were running in tight, crisscross patterns, narrowly missing each other, the noise of the wind rushing over their sails urgent and fearsome.

Rachel watched Marque, anticipating his next order, his calm and deliberate actions that of someone in complete control. His eyes constantly scanned the sails above them, trusting Alain to judge the speed and distance of the fast-approaching vessels on their leeward side.

Marque took them on a long tack high upwind, leaving the chaos of other yachts behind. The urgent shouts of crewmembers, followed by the wrenching crash when two yachts collided, sounded behind them.

Rachel glanced back and inhaled sharply at the sight of the fatally entangled yachts, the crew desperately working to restore order. One crewmember had been flung into the churning waters, and a bright orange lifebuoy flew in a slow arch toward him through the air.

"Ready to tack!" Marque's booming warning came, and Rachel readied herself for the sudden change in wind and direction that would come when Marque spun the wheel. The tack was completed cleanly and sharply. She glanced up, looking for the racing committee's boat on their starboard side. With some irritation,

Rachel noted how far they had traveled on their last run.

Too far. We've gone too far.

The run back to the starting line seemed too long a distance to cover before the gun would sound the start. Marque's gaze danced on the digital readouts of the instrument panel before a small smile rose to his lips.

Rachel glanced toward Alain who stood proudly at the mast, one hand loosely on the stay, his head thrown back as he stared toward the tip of the mast, reading the power over the sail with an expert's eye.

"More on the main!" Alain ordered from his position, and Rachel worked the winch to take in a couple of turns. She glanced up at the white carbon sheet, pulled flat and tight as a wing, and waited for Alain's response.

"One more!" his sharp request came to her. Rachel swore softly and leaned her whole body into the winch to take in one more turn against the force of the wind on the sail. The sound of the wind rushing over the tight sail whistled madly in her ears.

They picked up a knot. Then one more.

She glanced ahead and smiled in silent admiration at the distance they had covered. *Pure Joy* thundered down toward the starting line, her brilliant white sails taut as steel, the aerodynamic bow slashing through the water, throwing white spray high into the air. Rachel glanced frantically at the clock, but at the instant the gun boomed, *Pure Joy* crossed the line in full flight. Marque had timed it to perfection.

Alain turned and watched Rachel as she tightened the main line at his instruction, her body crouched low and balanced over the winch. Wet spray glistened on her bare legs, but she seemed oblivious to that, focusing all her efforts on the task of tightening the mainsail. She paused and stared up at the mast, her eyes burning with concentration, judging the effect on the sail.

Intrigued, Alain watched the beating pulse of her racing heart throbbing in her neck, visible just below her jaw line.

A tiny line of perspiration ran slowly down from behind her ear, down the curve of her neckline and over the hollow of her collarbone, plastering a few strands of hair against the wetness of her skin.

He blurred as the impulse tore at his loins—the impulse to run his tongue up the saltiness in her neck toward her ear and to bite her softly on the earlobe. He imagined her pinned on her back, his hands on her wrists, and she looked up at him, laughter dancing in her eyes, teasing him.

He leaned into her, ran his warm lips down her neckline, and she jolted with pleasure as he touched his lips to her neck. His tongue teased her soft skin, sensing the flutter of her rushed heartbeat. He noticed his own slow arousal and she moaned when he traced his tongue down her chest, deeply inhaling her sweet aroma.

"Prepare spinnaker!" Marque's brusque warning shocked Alain back to reality. He shot Marque's smiling face a daggered look and turned his attention to the horizon, seeking out all the telltale signs of currents or shifting winds.

Marque had taken them on a long, downwind tack, away from the fleet. They were running with the stronger wind, but had a longer leg to sail, and some of the other lighter yachts had gained on them.

Alain made a quick study of the wind speed and hooked the lanyard onto one of the three spinnakers they had selected for the race. When they turned downwind, he was ready, and with Christophe's assistance, they raised the spinnaker in a smooth, well-drilled move. In one slow, controlled balloon of bright red, the massive sail majestically filled with wind, surging the vessel downwind on the next leg.

*

Rachel watched as Alain heaved with his full strength on the spinnaker line, the sinewy muscles in his roped forearms rippling in the sun. His dark hair, wet from the sea spray, was plastered to his high forehead. His powerful body moved with catlike agility as he reached up high, and then pulled hard on the line, the shadow of the massive red sail momentarily blocking out the sun when it ran up the mast in one smooth, silent motion.

With quick, strong fingers, Alain secured the line onto a cleat and took a small step backward to study the wind on the sail. His deep chest heaved rhythmical from the exertion where he stood, head tilted back, his strong back arched. His skin glistened from the wet spray on his arms, biceps rippling as he held onto the mast for balance.

A deep urge stirred in her at the thought of Alain's hands stroking down her back, pulling her closer. She shuddered involuntary at the memory of his skillful tongue, teasing her to the point where she would cry out with anticipation and a need for more. She swallowed hard and glanced at Marque, guilty. If he had noticed anything, she was none the wiser, as Marque was staring out ahead, his eyes on the horizon with a shrewd smirk playing on his lips.

Six hours later, after they tacked for the final run on the homeward leg, *Pure Joy* had pulled out a ten-boat lead on the small group of chasing frontrunners. With the stronger wind blowing on her starboard side, no one could catch them. Rachel glowed in the euphoria and excitement of winning when they sailed back into the marina and headed for their berth.

*

Alain remained on the yacht long after they had moored *Pure Joy* and stowed her sails, and long after the last of the crewmembers disappeared to enjoy a deserved hot shower. He stood at the bow, in deep thought, arms crossed on his chest, absorbing the gentle sway of the vessel. His dark eyes were restless, flicking across the horizon, tinged with an angry red as the sun finally settled below the skyline.

Then he raised his hands and crossed them behind his head and sighed, relieved. He had changed his mind—Rachel would be his. Not just for one night, but for as long as they lived.

She was everything he desired, and he was prepared to face the consequences. He would face her husband, openly stating his intentions. It would not be done by a written note—not like his mother did it. But first, he must convince Rachel of his love, and given how he had treated her that might be an uphill battle.

With an easy motion, Alain stepped from the yacht onto the jetty to join the others in the clubhouse.

Chapter Twenty-One

Boisterous laughter and lively music filled the lounge at the St. Tropez yacht club. The room was packed with groups of people, their animated discussions drowning the sound of the background music. The mood was festive, while anxious servers ran around in their efforts to fill the glasses of the thirsty crowd. A journalist and her photographer prowled amongst the throng, eager to interview the class winners and shoot a photo of them brandishing their trophies.

Rachel tried her cocktail, and, finding it to her taste, sat back in her chair, crossing her legs. After the excitement and the demands of the day competing in the strong winds, she'd happily returned to her hotel room where she enjoyed a long, hot bath. She returned to the festivities at the yacht club refreshed, and was now enjoying the jovial camaraderie of the people with whom she had shared today's tough racing.

Her eyes drifted to where Alain stood, one shoulder leaning against a pillar on the far side of the room, deep in casual conversation with the skipper of the yacht that had chased them hard all day long. His arms crossed lightly over his chest, he was relaxed and confident.

She had noticed Alain surreptitiously watching her every move on the yacht today. Was he judging her? Testing her, to see if she passed the grade? Did he doubt her ability as a crewmember? She hated the idea of him judging her capabilities, and remembered with satisfaction the words of congratulations from Marque and the other crew when they finally docked in the harbor after the race.

At that moment, the female journalist interrupted Alain's discussion with the skipper, and Rachel's mouth tightened when the reporter placed her hand possessively on Alain's forearm and started interviewing him.

Rachel flipped her hair over her shoulder and turned her back on Alain to participate in the discussion at their table. Marque had the group in stitches with his dry recounting of the story about the club's commodore and his secret mistress. Apparently, his yacht *Tres Bonne* was frequently used for adventures other than the ocean-going type.

*

Alain cut the interview with the journalist short and returned to their table. He was delighted and secretly a little relieved to see Rachel had joined them for the rest of the evening.

He took a seat at their table and studied her across the short distance. She looked remarkably invigorated, her skin glowing, sun-kissed from the day on the open ocean. The silk strapless dress she wore complemented the sensual lines of her body. A single, brilliant cut, white diamond pendant hung on a delicate chain from her neck, the glittering brilliance of the stone inviting his attention to the slight cleavage of her breasts. She reached for her drink, took a small sip from the glass, and turned her gaze to meet Alain's burning eyes on her.

A light jolt passed through him as they locked eyes across the table. He tried to read her emotions, but she held his gaze without giving away anything. He resisted the sudden urge to reach for her hand on the table.

"You did well today."

She accepted his compliment with a nod and raised her glass to him. "Ditto," she replied and sat back.

"Can we go for a walk?"

Rachel held his gaze for a long moment, and then, without a word, they both stood. They left the warm, merry atmosphere of laughter, music, and clinking glasses, and stepped out into the fresh night air, the strong smell of the sea blown in from the Mediterranean by a light wind.

In a comfortable silence, they started walking, heading toward the pier. Rachel turned her face to the ocean and the soft, cool wind briefly lifted her hair before it fell back onto her shoulders again. Alain paused and cleared his throat.

"Rachel, I want us to start over." His was voice low and sure.

Rachel looked up, but he struggled to read her emotions. His eyes searched her face, waiting for her response. The wind ruffled his hair, and a loose twist fell over his forehead. He brushed it away with his right hand and stepped closer.

"Why?" she asked, the simple question causing him to pause, his jaw clenched. He was facing a crucial juncture with that question and thought about all the ways to answer it. His mind raced in search of the right answer. He briefly imagined what it would be like to leave her tonight and never see her again, and a crushing feeling suffocated him.

Running his hand through his hair, Alain continued, "I'm tired of trying to stay away from you Rachel, and . . . " he said with sudden realization, the sincerity thick in his voice. He paused, a little surprised by the frankness of his response.

"And I miss you when I'm not with you," he continued, staring down into the pools of her eyes, the urge to put his arms around her and hug her tight to his chest suddenly overwhelming.

"That evening in Monaco," he continued, haltingly, "I overreacted — have some issues from my past . . . "

"I know. Let's forget about it. Eugene told me about your mother."

Alain narrowed his eyes at her words. She had apparently earned Eugene's trust. *How can I win her trust?* Rachel turned to continue their walk.

Alain gently touched her elbow, urging her to stay. "There's more."

"I never wanted this to happen—but I've fallen in love with a married woman. I just want to be with you. I've felt this way ever since we met, and I don't—"

"*Was* married."

"I don't want . . . " Alain stopped mid-sentence at the shock of the words she had just whispered.

"Was married? But you told me—"

"I was married at the time. But you stormed from my room like a mad man. No *buts, ifs,* or *ands,* remember?" She smiled, but he noticed the hurt of the memory in her eyes.

Alain's arms dropped heavy and lifeless to his side. He exhaled long and slowly.

"When we met in Monaco, I had been separated for almost three years. My divorce was finalized shortly after I returned to London," she explained. "He disappeared into Africa, so it took a while to get divorced," she added, shrugging matter-of-factly.

Alain watched her in stunned silence. He gathered himself and with a slight edge in his voice implored, "Why, in all this time, haven't you told me?"

Rachel inhaled deeply. "At first I was angry—you were arrogant and judgmental."

Alain searched her face, and then asked, "And then, after that, when you figured out the reason for my behavior—why did you not tell me then?"

She turned to face the harbor, and replied, her eyes searching the far horizon, "I tried, Alain . . . after Cassis. But you were not interested . . . so cold. I couldn't deal with your rejection."

"I had to—I had to find a way to control my emotions," he replied.

"I wanted to tell you . . . tell you about my divorce, and that Stuart has not been part of my life for so long—" she added softly.

"Stuart is the father of the twins?" Alain asked gently.

"Yes, but fatherhood didn't suit him. He left us when they were six weeks old."

"Why?" This time the simple question came from Alain, and she didn't back away from his hand gently touching her shoulder.

"When we were young, love was easy. We had a carefree life. Then injury put an end to his tennis career. At the time the twins were born he was trying a new career. I guess he panicked—maybe the responsibilities brought on by the twins—I don't know . . . "

Alain watched while Rachel recounted the painful memories of her short marriage, strangely relieved at the absence of sadness or bitterness in her voice. She had put it behind her.

"And you've been raising the twins on your own since then?" he asked in a gentle voice.

"Yes, and I would not want to change that for anything."

"Never?"

"No," she said, brushing a wisp of hair from her face. "What I meant was that raising them on my own has been a good thing. I think they have been better off without Stuart. I don't want them hurt."

"And Stuart, does he not want to know them?"

"He made that decision long ago. He never bonded with Iain and Mia, and I was a fool for not understanding. To him, the twins were just a burden." Then, in a low voice, her eyes burning fiercely, she continued, "To me, they are everything."

Alain nodded. "I understand, but would you allow me to show you how I feel . . . trust me to be part of your life?"

Rachel studied his face in silence, a serious little frown on her forehead.

"Alain, is that really what you want? I'm the mother of two kids who mean the world to me. Our relationship thus far has been an emotional rollercoaster. I don't want to be hurt again." She dropped her gaze. "You're a carefree, attractive, single man. There are many other women you could pick that would suit your lifestyle much better." In a matter-of-fact voice she continued, "I don't think we should take this further."

Her words stung like hell. He wanted to correct her, but she turned and started walking down the pier toward her hotel.

"I will not give up—she's mine," he muttered softly, and with a few long strides, he fell in next to Rachel. They were silent until they reached her hotel.

"You're cold?" he asked, but she just shook her head. Alain removed his jacket and draped it gently over her shoulders.

The streets were quiet at that late hour in the sleepy part of the town. Rachel stood on the first step to the stairs leading up to the hotel entrance, her head level with Alain. He looked up to the building, shook his head, and smiled knowingly.

"Probably not a good thing if I walk you to your room. Remember what happened last time?" Embarrassment flushed briefly to her cheeks, but she said nothing.

"Rachel, you don't understand." Alain stepped closer. "I've made up my mind. I want you in my life—I *need* you in my life." He rested his hands on her shoulders. "And that includes Iain and Mia—give me an opportunity to show you."

*

A light charge rippled through her at his touch. She inhaled the sensual, manly smell of his warm body. Alain's burning eyes scanned her face for any signs of her emotions, but Rachel dropped her gaze to shield the deep, hidden need slowly awakening in her. She was betrayed by the slight shudder of her hands resting lightly on Alain's biceps.

His hand touched the skin of her cheek, and then, slowly, he raised her head with a tender finger under her chin to meet his gaze. She lifted her eyes to his, and she froze, catching her breath at the intensity of his eyes.

He pulled her closer, wrapping strong arms around her, and Rachel leaned her head on his chest. She closed her eyes at the warmth of his body, listening to the strong beat of his heart.

"Alain—"

"Ssshhh . . . .let me show you how we'll take this further." He silenced her gently and lowered his head, his lips stroking her forehead tenderly. She looked up at him and his mouth found hers, his tongue probing softly. A hushed sigh escaped her. Tension dissipated from her body as Rachel relaxed, and she leaned back in his arms, enjoying the soft touch of Alain's hand on her throat. His tongue skimmed the inside of her warm mouth, flicking over her teeth.

A soft moan came from her when he pulled her closer, and her breasts hardened. With more urgency, his tongue swirled in her mouth, warm and smooth, searching for more, and she gasped, dizzy from lack of air.

The world spun uncontrollably as he pressed his hard torso against her, his arousal strong and warm against her thigh. Her eyelids fluttered helplessly, painting flashes of hot red and white, and she grabbed a fistful of his black hair to steady herself. She shifted her lower body, grinding into Alain, the hot closeness of his sex driving her to bite on his lower lip.

Alain sucked in his breath at the unexpected pain, and with his right hand grabbed Rachel's upper thigh and pulled her upwards into him. Her body arched, and her head flopped back, leaving him to explore her neck, nibbling softly on her skin. His jacket slid from her shoulders to the ground. Shivers of pleasure rippled in waves down her body and she groaned again, this time with more passion.

The sound of the bell in the clock tower exploded above them, loudly ringing once. Rachel's eyes shocked wide open and she breathed in sharply, letting her hand slide down Alain's back and stepping out of his embrace.

"It's late." Her voice was shaky and heavy with lust. "You'd better go."

"You're killing me here, Rachel," Alain replied hoarsely. Clearing his throat, he demanded, "When can I see you again?"

She picked up Alain's forgotten jacket from the stone steps and held it out to him. "Well, you're driving me back tomorrow morning, aren't you? And you always know where to find me on Monday," she added with a playful smile and stepped back slowly as she started making her way up the stairs to the hotel entrance.

"No—you know what I mean." He groaned deeply.

Rachel looked down at the magnificent being standing at the foot of the stairs, jacket draped casually over his shoulder, wearing an inviting smile.

"Want to come for dinner?" she challenged him.

"Yes . . ." he responded quickly, and then suggested carefully, " . . . then I can also spend time with the kids."

"You'll have to be there early then," she warned him, almost at the top of the stairs.

"Won't miss it for anything in the world."

"Tomorrow evening, six o'clock."

Alain smiled brightly, turned and headed back in the direction of the yacht harbor.

Chapter Twenty-Two

He looked up to see the petite figure of a little girl walking carefully down the stone steps toward him—one step at a time. She was dressed in a bright yellow summer dress, billowing out from her hips and reaching just below her knees. A single, printed blue flower on her chest added a colorful touch, and her hair was pinned back with a collection of decorative floral pins.

At her heels followed two large Beaucerons, their pink tongues lolling from the side of their mouths in the heat. She came to a stop next to his vehicle. Alain leaned forward, tilting his head to look at her from under the Maserati's low roofline.

"You're Alain," she said with remarkable assertiveness for her age.

"Correct. And you must be Mia." He smiled, wondering where this was going.

"And you're visiting us?" she asked keenly.

"Yes, I am. Your mother invited me for dinner."

"Oh, yes, now I remember."

Alain waited patiently for her next prompt. She knitted a little frown, suddenly considering something important.

"I'll control the dogs. They can bite, you know." Her head bobbed to stress the importance of the situation.

"Thank you. We definitely don't want that to happen." The Beaucerons were watching, lying panting and uninterested in the heat.

"I'll show you," she announced with enthusiasm and turned to the two dogs. One hand on her hip, assuming the position of a strict schoolteacher, she raised a little index finger in the air.

"Sit, Romeo, sit!" she exclaimed in a commanding voice, bending forward at the hips to emphasize the command. Romeo sat up obediently and tilted his giant head sideways, waiting for her next command. With equal success, she repeated the same instruction to the bitch, Juliet. She turned to Alain, her head raised high with the satisfaction of her accomplishment. "See, they listen to me."

"I'm impressed," he nodded approvingly. "Is it safe to get out of the car now?"

Several affirmative nods assured his safety. Alain removed a wooden crate of rosé wine from the trunk and turned to see Rachel waiting at the front door, smiling down at them. The late sun touched her hair and the spaghetti strap dress caressed her figure with a sensual promise.

"You've been watching us," Alain complained, climbing the steps. "Left me hanging in the wind out there." He kissed her cheek and willed himself not to nip her ear. At the brief touch of his lips against her skin, he took in the sensual aroma of perfume.

"You did just fine."

Rachel turned, and Alain followed her to the back garden where Arianne was watching over Iain frolicking in the swimming pool. They moved to the arrangement of comfortable, pillowed deck chairs in the shade of the covered porch and sat down.

Iain noticed Alain and, suddenly losing all interest in swimming, he ran up to Alain, wet and shivering from spending the afternoon in the pool.

"Did you bring the Arati?" he asked wide-eyed, his teeth clattering uncontrollably.

Alain grabbed a dry towel and pulled the shivering body closer. Drying him vigorously, he replied, "Yeah, I brought the 'Arati.'" He looked up at Rachel and shrugged, surrendering to the fact that his powerful vehicle had been renamed forever.

"Time for a warm bath . . . Mia, Iain—" and with that Arianne coaxed the two unwilling bodies toward the house, their complaints and protestations echoing loudly as they made their way to a hot bath.

"You have two beautiful kids, Rachel."

"Thanks. They can be a handful at times. I don't know how I

would have managed without Arianne."

He scratched Romeo behind the ear. "The dogs came with you from London?"

She laughed. "No, they pretty much come with the house. They belong to Luke and Tina."

Alain sat back, his long legs stretched out in front of him, crossed at the ankles.

"They've been so good to me, especially after Stuart left . . . " Her voice trailed off.

"You did a great job on the renovation," Alain changed the topic comfortably. For his tact, Rachel awarded him a quick smile.

"Thanks. Eugene would agree with you—I used it as one of my references in our proposal for the chateau renovation."

Rachel stood and extended her hand in invitation to Alain. "Come, let's get inside. I'm going to tuck the kids in before I make our meal. Hope you like salmon."

"I'll cook," Alain said with confidence.

She stared at him skeptically. "I'm waiting for the punch line . . . "

"You go see to Mia and Iain . . . Go on, then. Don't you trust me in the kitchen?" With a playful pat on her derriere, he shooed her off in the direction of the kids.

Alain stepped into the kitchen, poured himself a glass of cold Chablis, took a slow, appreciative sip, and made a quick study of the layout—spice racks, utensil drawers, shelves for the heavy copper pots and pans.

All well laid out.

He opened the fridge and removed fresh salmon, dill, a bunch of thick, yellow asparagus, and a crisp green salad. Tapping his finger on the open door, he pondered the content of the fridge, and then added some plum tomatoes, a chunk of Parmesan cheese and an avocado to his stash. Lastly, he lit the two large candles on the marble-topped kitchen island.

*

When Rachel returned to the kitchen, Alain was busy adding salt to the wild rice simmering in a deep, copper-bottomed pot. "Your wine." He passed her a glass of the cold Chablis and pointed to the stool at the kitchen island. "Sit," he invited. "You're to do nothing but enjoy the meal tonight."

"This is a first for me." She laughed and took a seat.

"No man has ever cooked for you?" Alain asked in mock surprise.

"No, not unless I paid for it—" Then, at the mischievous grin on his face, she added quickly, "Like in a restaurant."

"Oh, don't be mistaken—you will pay for this meal tonight."

A soft, warm glow came to her cheeks and she returned his smile over the rim of her glass.

"Kids asleep?"

"Hmmm . . . "

Rachel lowered her head to her chest and massaged the back of her neck, enjoying the relaxed atmosphere in the kitchen and the ease with which Alain was preparing their meal.

He stepped toward her and, moving her hand, gently squeezed the stubborn muscles at the base of her neck. His hands were warm and strong, and the gentle pressure he exerted slowly relaxed the tension in her neck and back.

"They're working you too hard over at the chateau, aren't they?"

"They're absolute monsters. I will have to bump my fees soon."

The bubbling rice called for attention, and Alain returned to the stove to focus on the task of cooking. She watched with interest as he went about in the kitchen, his designer blue jeans a perfect fit over his narrow hips and the strength of his muscled thighs. He had rolled the sleeves of his white cotton shirt to his elbows, and the taut rope of muscles in his forearms danced in the candlelight. Her eyes came to rest on the tapered shape of his back while he poached the asparagus and prepared the salad with ease and practiced skill.

"Where did you learn to cook?" she asked, her voice slightly hoarse.

"Mostly self-taught," and then as an afterthought, he added, " . . . and Italy, of course."

"Please tell," she encouraged, sensing a good story.

"Italy, 1997," he started, his voice imitating an old man sharing a forgotten tale. "The mighty Giovanni family—devastated."

Rachel shifted in her chair, excited and preparing herself for a good story.

"'Our dear daughter, Claudina, will never get herself a good husband—her cooking is so very, very bad. Maybe we should try the cooking school in Tuscany.'"

Alain turned to her, leaning his right hip against the stove, arms crossed. "I saw her at the town market one morning, buying fresh produce for her cooking class. I desperately wanted to meet her." His eyes glinted with naughtiness. "So, I enrolled at the same cooking school, hoping to dazzle her with my French accent." A light shrug of his broad shoulders. "After wasting six weeks in cooking school, I eventually had to give up—she was of the good Catholic type."

She nodded, strangely relieved at how the story ended.

"But you learned something from that, did you not?" Rachel indicated the meal he was preparing on the stove.

"Yes. If you don't succeed after two weeks, walk away."

She grabbed a dishtowel and tossed it at him.

"You're impossible."

Alain tasted a drop of olive oil on his finger before he poured it over the salad in a large wooden bowl. Then he tossed the fresh tomatoes, avocado, and greens.

"Rice is about ready," he announced after checking the texture of the grain. "How do you like your salmon?" Then he leaned over and touched his lips gently to the skin of her neck, just below her ear. A soft ripple of pleasure ran down her spine, and she tilted her head, exposing the delicate skin of her neck to his lips.

"Suddenly I don't feel like cooking anymore."

"Then I'll just have to stop tempting the chef," she replied and pulled away reluctantly.

Alain returned his attention to preparing their meal. Soon he had the salmon cooked to perfection, and they sat down to enjoy his efforts.

"Mmmm," Rachel exclaimed at the first bite. "Very, very tasty, Mr. Léon. You're a man of many hidden talents."

*

Alain nodded with a smile, but the taste of the meal was wasted on him. For him, the evening held a delectable promise for satisfying a different type of hunger.

"Dessert?" Rachel asked when they had finished their meal, and when Alain declined with a silent shake of his head, she added in a low voice over her shoulder as she stepped to the fridge, "Fresh strawberries and cream—sure you don't want any?"

The lingering promise in her voice made Alain think twice about her offer. She placed the bowl of fruit and thick cream on the table and slowly lifted her gaze to Alain. The soft candlelight danced inviting shadows on the honey-brown of her skin

"No?" she asked again, dipping a juicy strawberry into thick clotted cream and offered it to him. His chest tightened, and Alain leaned forward for Rachel to place the aromatic fruit in his mouth. Then Alain picked a bright red strawberry from the bowl and dipped it slowly into the cream. Rachel closed her eyes and Alain offered her the delicious fruit. She parted her lips and slowly licked the soft white cream from her mouth. Alain watched, mesmerized, unconsciously holding his breath.

She opened her eyes slowly, and Alain read the warm promise in the glowing amber flashes. He reached to lay his hand gently on her cheek and touched his lips tenderly to her mouth. Then he inhaled deeply and closed his eyes in desire at her smell.

"So, what do I owe you for the meal tonight?"

He nibbled softly on her earlobe in answer. "Oh, I have something special in mind."

"Tell me," she demanded in a husky voice, closing her eyes.

He pulled her closer and parted her lips with his tongue. She responded willingly, his tongue darting around in her mouth.

With one swift movement, Alain swooped his arms under Rachel and picked her up, their lips still locked. Rachel gasped as he lifted her and flung her arm around his neck.

"Where?" He could muster only the single word, his voice suddenly hoarse.

She pointed toward a door, and he carried her to the main bedroom where he lowered her slowly onto the bed. He paused briefly while she fumbled in the dark with the lamp on the nightstand. A click and then a soft glow filled the room.

Her wet lips glistened invitingly in the soft light, and he dropped his hand to slowly lower the strap of her dress from her shoulder. She looked up into his eyes, and he saw the embers glow brighter, deep in her eyes. She lifted her shoulder and the other strap slipped off, revealing the soft, white skin of her breasts. Slowly he traced the sensuous contour of her breast with his tongue.

"Take me in your mouth," she whispered, and he responded with eagerness, sucking on her hardened nipple. He craved for the touch of her nakedness against his skin, wanting nothing between their bodies, and raised his arms above his head. She reached up with one easy tug she removed his shirt.

He lifted Rachel's torso, and, as he slipped her dress from under her, she started ripping at the buttons of his jeans. They fell in a tangle of naked limbs on the bed, heaving at the closeness of their bodies.

*

The shock of their sudden nakedness rushed through Rachel's veins. Alain leaned forward and touched her lower ribcage with his mouth, blowing softly on her skin. She shuddered at the pleasure thrills running down her spine, hot like fire. With a wicked sense of knowing, he ran the tip of his tongue slowly down her quivering belly, drawing a long, soft moan from her.

Then, a fierce desire to please Alain came over Rachel. She sat up and pulled his head back to her face, whispering, "Wait, I want to please you."

Pushing her hands against his muscular chest, she forced him back onto the bed to lie on top of him. With wicked patience, she ran the tip of her tongue down his heaving chest, her naked body sliding down on his. His erection strained mightily, and she paused, gently teasing him with her hardened breasts. Alain groaned softly, lying spread-eagled on the bed, his eyes wide, fixed into space.

Rachel slithered down lower onto his hard, flat stomach, plucking gently with her lips on the thin line of dark, curly hair that ran invitingly from his navel. She wet her lips and touched his arousal—barely, then blew soft, warm air onto it.

Alain groaned aloud and his hard, jagged breathing stuttered and stopped. His body stalled—quivering, straining as if against some powerful, unseen force. Desire flamed bright in his dark eyes, yet Rachel waited a moment longer. Then, unexpectedly, she took his full erection deep into her mouth.

With a mighty heave, Alain's breath exploded from his lungs. His pelvis thrust upward forcefully.

"Enough!" he shuddered and grabbed a handful of Rachel's hair. She looked up and smiled at him, shaking her head slowly from side to side. This was her turn to please him. She wanted it this way.

With one smooth movement, Alain grabbed her and spun her around, pinning her helplessly underneath him. Rachel shrieked and laughed with joy. The strong weight of Alain's hard body sunk down onto her as he pushed her back against the luxurious goose-down pillows.

"Protection," she whispered with a mischievous smile on her lips. Alain leaned over Rachel, his chest delicious and heavy on her, while he fished a foil-wrapped condom from his jeans on the floor. Fascinated, her eyes transfixed on his hands, Rachel watched as Alain unrolled the condom over him.

"Slowly," she whispered when he turned to her, and he gently nipped her neck, burying his face in her hair. She searched for his hand and placed it gently on her breast, squeezing softly. Alain inhaled sharply and lowered his head to her breast, his warm mouth sucking, nibbling on her swollen nipple.

Rachel ran her hand down his back, and as he moved above her, she traced the ripples of hard muscle that crisscrossed his back. The firm smoothness of his skin came alive under her touch, and deliberately, she raked her nails slowly down his back, enjoying the accomplishment of her action. Her hand came to rest on his tight, round buttocks and she pushed down on the smooth firmness. He arched his body majestically above her, threw his head back, and split her open with his thighs. His massive arousal was hot and hard against her skin.

Oh, I want him—right now, inside me.

Rachel looked up at Alain, deep lust drifting like smoke over his eyes. She hooked her limbs around his narrow hips, drawing him closer to her, into her—teasing him, laughing.

In a swift movement, Alain gripped her wrists in one powerful hand, pinning them above her head on the pillow, leaving her exposed and vulnerable under him. She reveled at the controlled power of his grip, lying defenseless on her back, watching his dark, smoldering eyes. He lowered slowly to take a ripe, swollen nipple in his mouth, and with his other arm reaching under her back, arched her body upwards to him.

Rachel tightened her legs on Alain's manly body as he ground his pelvis against her, his arousal big, hard, and urgent. She tilted her hips slightly, wanting him in her.

Teasingly, carefully, mindfully, he touched her with his hard arousal. Then, gently, he entered her wetness, shallow at first. His body froze in space when Rachel gasped sharply at his initial entry, her body tensed like steel wire at the unfamiliarity of accommodating him.

It had been a while.

They both waited. Quivering.

She held her breath, waiting for her body to relax, to accept his hot, delicious shaft. The muscles in Alain's powerful back rippled under her hand and his breathing came in ragged rasps as he hovered above her, allowing her the time to take him deeper into her.

Rachel's body began to relax, safe in the knowledge that he was waiting for the first, slow thrust of pelvis to come from her. Carefully, testing, she thrust her pelvis upwards, letting him drive deeper into her wet warmth. And then Alain began to move in slow, grinding circles, matching her.

Rachel's body tingled with anticipation, and she thrust upward to meet Alain, slowly at first, and then with more urgency, their rhythm building, becoming deeper and harder, their bodies locked in unison. Her breathing became rushed with a warm, deep desire spilling over her, blanking her mind from everything but the need for Alain to thrust inside her, deeper.

The world began to spin, slowly at first, then wilder and faster, and she thrashed her head from side to side, willing their bodies together as they gyrated in locked passion. Her vision blurred, and she could smell the muskiness of their lust grow stronger, and then, suddenly, the need to be closer to him was so overpowering that she smashed and ground herself against Alain's hard pubic bone with an almost frantic urgency.

Incredibly, a forgotten, hidden sensation of pleasure, dormant for years, slowly ascended from deep inside her, lifting her, driving her body to spasm powerfully into a long, beautiful arch. Sensation tore from her body like hot, molten lava.

Rachel's deep inhalation burst from her lungs in an explosive gasp, and she cried out loudly at the peak, vaguely aware of the deep, roaring bellow escaping from Alain's chest.

His upper body shuddered with his own exploding orgasm, and he let go of her wrists, throwing his head back and lifting his powerful upper torso high, the muscles in his neck straining like oiled steel cords. Wet hair was plastered in dark curls on his forehead, and his heaving chest glistened a deep, shiny gold, like an ancient god in the soft light.

As Alain opened his eyes, she tilted her head and watched with fascination as the focus slowly returned to his dark pupils. He gingerly lowered himself onto his elbows, taking most of his weight onto his shoulders and upper arms, and brushed a long wisp of hair from her face. A thin line of perspiration trickled down her neck, and he ran his tongue over it gently.

"You are so beautiful," he whispered, his deep voice a soft rumble against her ear.

She smiled at him and laid her hand on his cheek.

*

Slowly, gently, Rachel became aware of the soft, early morning light of the rising sun and the welcome sound of mourning doves in the willow tree at the window. Her senses woke, and she opened her eyes lazily. A magnificent, bronze arm drifted slowly into focus.

With a slight start, she opened her eyes wider.

Alain.

He was on his side, naked, his head resting lightly on a supporting hand under his ear. A slight, dark shadow lined his strong jaw line. He reached out with his free hand and touched her tenderly on the cheek.

"Morning," he said softly, as if not to disturb her.

Rachel smiled and laid her hand on his, enjoying the warmth on her face.

"Hi," she whispered shyly.

His dark eyes probed hers, deep and intense.

"What?" she asked and cleared her throat, suddenly thirsty.

Alain turned to face her squarely, his mouth set in a serious line.

"What?" she repeated.

"I've never said this to a woman. I don't think I knew what it felt like before." She watched while Alain gathered his thoughts once more. "Rachel, I really love you—more than I ever knew possible."

Rachel closed her eyes to the warm tears of joy welling up.

Once again, Provence had been good to her.

Chapter Twenty-Three

Rachel paced through the refurbished chateau in slow, measured steps. The muted click of her heels on the reclaimed, wide-plank hardwood flooring echoed from the high, vaulted ceiling. Her gaze went over the carefully restored interior to take in the polished marble staircase, the heavy, crystal chandeliers, and the beautiful, ornate ceiling plaster moldings. The restoration work had been completed to such precision and high standards that, even subjected to her most critical inspection, she couldn't spot any defects.

Two large trucks rumbled noisily down the road and made their way toward the service entrance on the north side of the main building.

Satisfied, Rachel swirled one last time to take in the expanse of the impressive ballroom and then made her way to the front entrance, where she opened the heavy carved wooden door.

Alain's low-slung DB6 was slowly making its way up the newly paved driveway, flashes of bright sunlight reflecting off the sleek bodywork through the dappled lane of leafy plane trees. On his lap sat Iain, small hands gripped tightly on the steering wheel and his face drawn into a tight ball of concentration. In the passenger seat next to them, Mia sat, waving regally when they drove past an appreciative Eugene. She leaned her head lightly against the doorframe and smiled lovingly as her mind drifted to the events that led to this beautiful day.

Rachel was cautious in answering Alain's love at first, and watched with some trepidation as the bond between Alain and her children grew stronger by the day. With time, she had realized that Alain's love for her and her children was true and deep, and that she could trust him.

During the final weeks of the renovation project, she had some of the best days of her life. She and Alain had shamelessly neglected the project, sometimes for days, to enjoy the last of the warm summer days with the kids. Alain's long string of excuses to take the kids on excursions such as swimming at Baie De Pampelonne, or picnic lunches on Porquerolles, or endless boat trips on his yacht, still made her smile.

Then, as soon as the first snow covered Mt. Blanc, Alain insisted they spend a week at his chalet in Megeve, where he enlisted the services of the world's finest ski instructors for the kids. After lunch, he would devote the afternoon to skiing with them, beaming at their progress. It was endearing to watch Alain on the gentle bunny slopes, skiing backwards in slow, wide turns, as he encouraged and urged Iain and Mia in their efforts.

Megeve would always have a special place in her heart. It was here, watching Alain with the kids, that she declared her love for him.

Finally, in early February, they finished the renovation project. Exactly two days after the completion of the renovation, Alain approached Rachel with a suggestion to join him for a couple of days "away from it all."

"Where would we go?"

"Oh, maybe somewhere in northern Europe," he replied vaguely.

"In February? Won't that be too chilly?"

"Wait and see." The mysterious smile on his face convinced her in a heartbeat.

To Rachel's surprise, she had increasingly found signs of Alain's mysterious hand in a number of the arrangements involving her life and that of the kids. When she called her parents on the Wednesday, she learned that they were on their way to Gatwick to catch a flight to Marseilles.

"Alain arranged it," her mother's voice echoed over the phone, heavy with conspiracy. Next she overheard Tina requesting Arianne to ready the guest cottage. "For your parents' visit . . . Alain arranged it."

Later that week, after their private flight had left Marseilles and leveled off at 33,000 feet, Rachel reclined her seat and turned toward Alain on her left.

"You've been so secretive," she sulked. "You've arranged all the travel plans, flew my parents down to take care of the twins—I only found out where we going a couple of minutes ago."

"That's all part of the element of surprise, isn't it?" Alain laughed, and nodded toward his trusted air hostess to serve the chilled champagne.

"But you would hardly let me pack any clothes . . . "

" . . . and by packing, you've now spoiled my plans to surprise you with a new wardrobe," Alain replied and shook his head in mock frustration.

From Marco Polo airport, a limousine scooted them to a wooden Spencer runabout waiting with running motors to skirt them over the water canals to their presidential suite at the luxurious Hotel Palazzo Vendramin.

Shortly after their arrival, Alain accompanied Rachel to a personal costume fitting where they selected and fitted their period costumes for the world famous Il Ballo del Doge. She could hardly contain her excitement, and Rachel's animated babbling raised much tongue clicking from the dress fitter as she struggled to get her job done.

That Saturday evening, Alain and Rachel arrived by private water transfer at the sumptuous Palazzo Pisani Moretta on the Grand Canal for the Venetian masked ball. A low buzz came from the admiring crowd as they stepped into the fairy-tale world of costumed jesters, dancers, acrobats, and daring fire-eaters. Rachel and Alain struck a regal pose in their lavish costumes as they gracefully descended the wide staircase. Hidden behind her mask, she could afford a quiet smile at the stir they had caused, and with her hand hooked into Alain's elbow, she silently pinched him on his arm.

By midnight, while the dancing was still in full swing, Alain took her by the arm and led her from the ballroom. It was surprisingly mild outside, and Rachel leaned her head happily against Alain's shoulder while they strolled down quiet, narrow streets. She sighed, satisfied at the feeling of happiness that cloaked her like a warm blanket as they walked along the water canals. Alain paused when they crossed the Rialto Bridge, and they turned to take in the sight of the full moon over the Venice skyline. For minutes, they stood in silence, taking in the image of the bell tower of St. Mark's Basilica in the distance, painted in a soft blue hue.

Then Alain turned and looked into her eyes.

"You happy, Rachel?" he asked, his dark eyes intense, searching her face.

"Very," she answered, not sure where he was going with this. He stood, quiet for a moment, his eyes still on her face.

"What?" she asked, trying the fathom his behavior.

Alain reached into his pocket, and when he opened his hand, he held a small, square box. Then, with infinite care, he laid his hand on her cheek. Rachel's heart fluttered wildly as she realized what was about to happen.

"It is impossible to love someone more than I love you." He paused for a moment before he continued. "Rachel Swift, will you marry me?" His words came to her over the soft gurgle of water under the Rialto Bridge.

When they returned to France two days later, Tina arrived in a cloud of dust at her front door within the hour, her excitement bordering on manic. They had a million arrangements to make in a very short time, and for Tina, nothing but absolute perfection would be acceptable. The venue was set at the newly renovated Chateau Léon.

*

Rachel pushed herself from the doorframe with a happy sigh and walked to meet Alain and the kids where they were parked in the shade. Iain saw her, and happy laughter rang out as he sprinted toward her open arms. She lifted him high in the air and swung him in a wide arch before setting him down. Arianne stepped from the chateau, and Iain ran up the stone steps to meet her. Mia, on the other hand, approached her in her newfound, more sedate, ladylike fashion.

"Mommy, I love the flowers." Mia pointed to the large, wooden arbor on the manicured lawn under the old willow tree, decorated with garlands of honeysuckle and willow. Large bouquets of fresh white lilies and long-stemmed roses framed the arbor to create a large, floral arch. Set along the center aisle were neat rows of pristine white wooden benches for the wedding guests. A thick-piled, red runner led to the polished mahogany pew in the front. Tina's hand was to be seen everywhere.

Inside, she had transformed the grand ballroom to its former glitzy splendor, and the massive room brimmed with stylishly decorated dining tables, heavy with crystal champagne flutes, white porcelain, and silver flatware. Massive bouquets of white roses and lilies competed with the elaborate silver candelabras and printed menus to decorate the tables.

A low stage had been erected on the far side to accommodate the five-piece band Tina had flown in from Vienna—it was the single aspect of all the wedding arrangements Tina simply refused to negotiate. It had to be this specific band.

At last count, Rachel had tallied just over six hundred confirmed guests. A small, Venetian glass replica of the chateau, neatly wrapped in white and silver, was placed at each seat as a token of thanks and goodwill.

Behind the high double doors leading from the ballroom, Chez Du Pont had annexed the dining room and most of the lounge to accommodate the row upon row of entrees, main courses and dessert that would be coming from his small army of staff in the kitchen.

Eugene had thrown open the ancient doors to his impressive wine cellar, and the twenty wine stewards, under the critical stare of Chateau Léon's head sommelier, eagerly awaited the event, dressed in their royal blue and white uniforms.

"Aren't you supposed to be manicured, or styled, or something?" Alain questioned and reached to give Rachel a long, warm hug.

"I just wanted to take one last look," she said, her voiced muffled against his chest.

"Nothing more to be done, Angel—it's all ready for the big moment."

She sighed. "And I wanted to see you."

Alain hugged her closer. His view drifted out toward the azure blue of the ocean in the hazy distance.

"Oh, no, what have I done wrong?" he asked lightly.

"I just wanted to say thank you. Thank you for loving me, and thank you for loving my kids."

She pushed herself back in his embrace to look up into his laughing dark eyes. "You've restored my faith in love."

ABOUT THE AUTHOR

Lieze Gerber is an emerging novelist who writes contemporary romance. Born and raised in South Africa, Lieze now calls Vancouver, Canada home. She studied law in South Africa, but lately, her love for writing has won the case against her practical side.

Lieze currently lives in France with her husband and two rather spoilt Scottish Terriers, where she is working furiously on the Love Restored trilogy. In her spare time, she likes to relax with her canvas and paintbrushes, or jump on her bicycle and hit the closest trail.

You can visit her online at *www.liezegerber.com.*

In the mood for more Crimson Romance? Check out *California Sunset* by Casey Dawes at *CrimsonRomance.com*.

www.ingramcontent.com/pod-product-compliance
Lightning Source LLC
Chambersburg PA
CBHW010642100726
47900CB00011B/2937